SIX BREEDS

"—she cleared the slashing fangs that whirled at her and slipped beneath the shield of her own sharp teeth." [see p. 207]

SIX BREEDS

by *RALPH G. KIRK*

With illustrations by
CHARLES
LIVINGSTON
BULL

Short Story Index Reprint Series

BOOKS FOR LIBRARIES PRESS
FREEPORT, NEW YORK

First Published 1923
Reprinted 1970

STANDARD BOOK NUMBER:
8369-3592-6

LIBRARY OF CONGRESS CATALOG CARD NUMBER:
70-125225

PRINTED IN THE UNITED STATES OF AMERICA

To
My Mother

Contents

Illustrations

Gun-Shy

"I've never met this skunk," Dan Thorplay told me, handing over the letter he had been rummaging after in his littered desk, "but I've got hopes." So you can lay a bet that the first thing I looked for on that sheet of paper was the signature.

"Yours cordially, M. Arrendale," the communication ended.

I know my share of polecats; but it so happens that none of them is named M. Arrendale; so, since the bottom of that letter gave me no inkling as to the story Dan was about to perpetrate, I started at the top. Here's how it went:

Mr. Dan Thorplay,
Field Trial & Gun Dog Trainer,
Sam Houston Inlet, Texas.

Dear Sir: I'm shipping my setter pup, Red Feather, U.S.K.A. 345726, clear from Ohio down to you. Holden says you're the best dog trainer in America. You'd better be, with the job you've got before you. Break my dog to the gun; quail. He's gun-shy. I tried to straighten him out the past season. Nearly tore his head off with the spikes; but no go. One more week and he'd have been steady to every noise but Gabriel's tooter. But the season closed, so he's still alive—somewhat; and still gun-shy.

Keep him till next quail time if you must. If you can't swing it by then I guess it can't be done. But don't shoot him if you fail. Send him back to me. I hanker to do that little job of killing my own way. Send the bills to me once a month.

Yours cordially, M. ARRENDALE.

"Seems like a lovable personality," I remarked, handing the paper back.

Dan Thorplay didn't smile, and that, I knew, though I hadn't finished my first two hours in his company, was the easiest thing he did. And so, not knowing Dan except, as you might say, by U. S. Mail, I got him wrong.

Five years ago, or thereabouts, a letter postmarked Texas, sliding through our door slot, up in Pennsylvania, had started another of those good friendships that are built on dogs. With much curiosity I had ripped the envelope.

I don't know bulldogs. I'm a bird-dog man. But my head is bare to courage. I liked that pit-fight story. The way those two dogs chopped each other up was something sweet and pretty.

Thus one Dan Thorplay, starting a desultory but delightful correspondence, with the result that here, at last, after five years I sat, loafing in Dan's big living room, a couple thousand miles from home—a half-hour guest with a Texas welcome warming me to

half-century intimacy. But, as I said, I got Dan
wrong first off. How was I to know on such a short
acquaintance that a faraway sad expression always
comes into Dan Thorplay's boy-blue eyes whenever
he is considering the desirability of bopping some one
on the snout? So, when he failed to smile, I re-
signed myself to tragedy.

Whenever some mighty spinner of yarns makes a
dog hero die I never forgive him. It's bad enough
that real dogs actually must go. But if the story is
one of sure enough facts I'm glad to face them.
There's consolation enough for me in the truth that
by their game and gallant deaths, dogs have done
even more to soften human hearts and make the
world a better halfway house than they have by their
game and gallant lives.

"Shoot us the works," I demanded, bold as a water
cracker, but with many misgivings, I'm afraid, in
my dog-loving heart. And Dan let go both barrels.

"I failed to look this bird-dog butcher up as I
should have—him or his pup," Dan started off—"so I
had no warning as to what was coming. Then, a
week later, I was sorry. Served me right.

"Andy MacAndrews called me up one day, from
the express office at Palacios. 'Bad news, boss,' said
Andy. 'You know that Arrendale pup you sent me in
for?'

" 'Sure,' I told him. 'Didn't find him dead in his
shipping crate, did you?'

" 'No such luck!' came Andy's voice, bright as a

bucket of casket varnish. 'He's only three-quarters dead. And he's a Gordon!'

"I made a few remarks about the dukes of the honourable old Scotch house of Gordon that had the insulation dripping off the wires all the way to Palacios. And Andy MacAndrews, despite his lineage, checked me on every word.

" 'Then I'll ship him back?' MacAndrews ventured hopefully over the wire. But I happened to need the money.

" 'No!' I roared back; and hung up on the sulphurous remarks that my helper was making about the very setter in which he should have taken a national pride."

Dan Thorplay scratched a match and pulled the little flame down into his pipe bowl several times.

"A Gordon setter is about the handsomest pup that grows," my host went on after the air about his head was properly beclouded. "The handsomest of the bird dogs, anyhow, beyond the slightest shadow of a doubt. Great, big, upstanding fellows with the bone of a colt and the furnishings of a Dane, and a face full of teeth to make a cougar shiver his whiskers loose. Coat black, black, black! No use to say 'as black as,' for you stop at the second 'as,' and there you are! The only comparison you can make regarding that fellow's colour is the other way about—'Black as a Gordon's coat'—say that, and you're telling the folks about something as far away from white as you can get.

"And lustrous! They try to tell me that white reflects the light, and that black absorbs it. But the fellow that said that never owned a Gordon setter. The light comes rushing to you off that Scotchman's silky jacket in waves and gleams and glints and sparkles and flames. Even his gorgeously red Irish cousin cannot match his coat. And the handsomest of English setters is dull and drab of raiment in comparison. And to set off the unbelievably dense jet of him, there outcrops here and there rich golden colour through the blazing blackness—spots and streaks of sharply outlined mahogany-tan that adorn his eyes and cheeks and throat and ears and the feather of his legs with the richest of contrasting-colour splashes. For looks he's a setter dog if ever there was a setter dog. But I wouldn't have one for a gift," snapped Thorplay, bringing his panegyric to a sudden and unexpected close.

"I'm the world's champion listener," I said, and waited.

"No class," Thorplay explained. "No class at all. And a mind of his own; Scotch. Too big. Too slow. Wrong colour against the deep shadows and russet-browns of autumn. Not wide enough. Potters about. No speed or range. A fat man's dog. Finds birds, but not with snap and ginger; and when he does, never knocks you stiff with the sheer kick in his points. Strong-headed; self-willed; hard to train; and after you have trained him, what? No class. And to cap it all, there isn't a bird-dog trainer in

America, bar one thick-skulled exception, who doesn't believe implicitly that the tan on a Gordon's back legs runs right on up till it hits his backbone, and follows that, getting wider and yellower every inch of the way till it strikes the base of his skull."

Dan retarded his spark. A cool breeze came drifting off the Gulf waters and tiptoed about the room. I wriggled deeper into the wolfhides. From somewhere in the back part of the house there came to my ears a soul-satisfying sound—the subdued clatter as of dishes and cups and saucers jogging elbows sociably. A cotton-thatched old darky scraping into the room threw a lighted match into the dried grass that made a carpet under the fireplace logs.

I could see that this was going to be a perfectly detestable evening.

"Gimme a match," said Dan.

I givvim.

" 'Barring one thick-skulled exception,' " I prompted my host complacently.

"That's me!" Dan stated, puffing a time or two. Then suddenly he blew up.

"Gun-shy!" he roared. The sudden explosion shot through the barrel of the old muzzle-loader Dan was pulling at. "Gun-shy!" And the sparks and ashes flew.

"That dog was gun-shy, whip-shy, man-shy, horse-shy, bird-shy, fur-shy, collar-shy, cord-shy, water-shy, wind-shy and rain-shy. The only thing in the wide, wide world he wouldn't scare at was his feed pan.

Poor little pup! I took one look at him cramped up there in the cruel half-size crate in which he had travelled all those miserable miles, and from that second on my knuckles have itched every time the name of Arrendale comes into my mind. Cringing and thin, bloodshot of eye and bloody of neck, twitching with partial paralysis from the spiked collar that in some murderer's hands had made a fly-blown mess of his one-time lovely throat, burs from the hunting season still in his coat, pads of his feet swollen to double size from the sand spurs that had never been removed and which Nature was trying to flush by suppuration from between his toes; broken and whimpering and sick and scared, he looked to me as though a merciful load of buckshot was the training he needed most. I thought I'd have to lift him out of his crate, he looked so weak and spiritless. I opened the door and called him. And he came creeping forth on his belly; a sight to sicken your heart at the thought that you belonged to a race of creatures including a member who could do such a thing to a setter dog. I stooped to pat him. I had left off work on a wonderful pointer pup that I had been teaching to retrieve; and the tools of the job were still about me; and when I bent over to give the little stranger a re-assuring rub the force collar fell out of my pocket and dropped on the ground in front of the late ar-rival. Whereupon, before I could move a hand to grab him, he became at once the late departed. One moment he was a pitiable slat-ribbed critter who apparently had not the strength to lift him to his feet. The next he was a fast-disappearing speck on the horizon's edge. He took one lightning glance at that spiked collar, and headed for New Mexico.

"Andy MacAndrews swung a long leg over the old cayuse whose principal calling in life is to run down bolting dogs. Many's the pup that has tried to match his wind and heels against that old mouse-gnawed roan—to return in an hour or two a sadder and wiser dog. But the moon was high that night before the Gordon dog came in, riding, if you please, across Andy's thighs.

" 'I drags him for half a mile,' says Andy. 'And then it filters through my thick skull that nothin's goin' to train this pup but lovin'. He's been through hell. I aim to meet the Piute that done this little thing.'

"And he put the bony fellow across my forearms.

" 'And, hoss,' says Andy, as he stood rubbing the old bronc's nose, 'we rambled. With the name I got' —and he turned to me—'I've always been a-lookin', secret-like, for some good points in the Scottish setter. Today I get results. Right this minute, boss, you got on your arms the widest-going bird hunter that ever came to Sam Houston Inlet. If that Gordon dog hadn't run into the north arm of the bay his first cast would have landed him in Santa Fé by sunrise.'

"For a month we attempted nothing. Just fed and doctored and petted him. Then started his yard training. This proved easy. The dog had brains, and he'd been through this before. But I went all over it again, but without the use of any of my tools. Collar and cord and whip into the discard; for not the slightest punishment could be used. It was a job; but we made the grade, and he came to know that training here was not synonymous with physical torture. And at last we got to the place where he obeyed his commands without cringing. Here was victory. For a long while he would try to bolt at sight of a collar, and failing to get away would turn all four up, like a dead horse, and tremble pitifully. But at last through endless patience and kindness we overcame even that, and arrived at the point where we could force him a bit; and having built his spirit up to the point where he could stand a little discipline we shook hands all around.

"We had come to the stage where it was up to us to try him out with the gun; and I dreaded it. Of all dog problems, gun-shyness is the thing most difficult of solution, the thing that takes the greatest forbearance and self-control and insight to the very soul of the dog. But at last I showed him a gun.

"We had him tied, of course, and had carefully closed all the gates to the yard; for to have him bolt and make a get-away then would be fatal. Good feeding and kind treatment had filled him out. He was right then the biggest setter I'd ever seen. And the strongest. And not done growing. I turned my back to him, and carelessly, as though the matter was devoid of interest to him, and none of his business whatever, I took a gun from behind his kennel and started across the yard with it, away from him. He saw it. His chain was strong and his collar stout, but the frantic leap he made jerked loose the heavy staple that fastened the end of his chain to the kennel. He made one lightning crazy dash for the training-yard fence. It's ten feet high. Yet he hooked his forefeet over the top strand of cattle wire and struggled over. And his dragging leash flipped round one of the strands of the fence, and held. And so he hung, choking and jerking and wild. I took him down, strangled and palsied with gun fear and force-collar fear, his returning confidence utterly destroyed. Three months' work gone to the devil. Gun-shy, collar-shy, trainer-shy. Except for physical condition he was the same dog that had streaked it across the prairie for Santa Fé a dozen weeks before.

"Well, we started in again. I never saw the dog I couldn't train. This time it took me half a year to get back to where we had been when I showed him the gun. And then I got a letter from up Ohio way, reminding me that the quail season was close at hand. But before I answered it I telegraphed Doc Holden. 'Who's Arrendale?' I wired. His answer came back at once: 'Litter brother to Bill Sikes. Letter follows.'

"Doc knows that one of my failings is Dickens, so I didn't need his letter; but I delayed writing to

Ohio, anyhow, until it came; and when it did I read things in it that largely influenced my reply to Arrendale. I wrote him:

"*Dear Sir:* Inclosed you'll find two checks. The one is for ten months' training charges herewith returned to you. I've fallen down. Whoever failed to break your dog of gun-shyness before he came down here, fixed him so that nobody else can fix him.

"The other check is open. Fill in the figures that seem fair to you and let me keep the dog. As far as being a bird dog is concerned, licking the pot is as far as he'll ever get. But a violent love affair has sprung up between your dog and my two-year-old kid; so we can't bear to have him sent back to be killed. Won't you please oblige us? Yours truly.

"I mailed the letter and then scurried into town and drew out all but four hundred dollars from my checking account and waited. Four hundred dollars is ten times what he paid for the pup. I looked that up. And twice the value of the best Gordon setter that ever pottered over a foot scent. But I was damned if I was going to send that setter back to Ohio.

"A few days later I very anxiously opened a letter from up north. You couldn't guess what was in it, Church, not in a hundred years. My check—filled in to the tune of twenty-five hundred smackers—and a letter, which I read as soon as consciousness returned. It went something like this:

"I have my doubts if a dog-trainer's bank account can stand a drag like this; but if it can, mail the check back to the bank mentioned below. It's indorsed for deposit. When the check's returned the setter is yours. The dog's not worth ten cents to me as a dog. But I happen to be wealthy and can afford to pay a high price for my amusements. If he's got you licked I guess I couldn't break him either; but I figure I'd get just twenty-five hundred dollars' worth of fun doing it—or else. Doubting that you can afford as much for your offspring's pleasure as I can for my own, I am

"Yours very cordially,
"M. ARRENDALE."

Dan Thorplay stopped his narrative long enough to pull a little gutta-percha whistle out of his pocket and give it a prolonged low blast.

"Now what would you have done in a case like that?" he asked me.

I shook my head. "You've got me stopped," I answered. "What did you do?"

And as though in reply there came a clicking on the porch door and in through an open window leaped as beautiful a thing as it has ever been my lot to see.

A setter dog as black as—and there, as Dan had warned, you are. A lot of sense there'd be in using some weak-kneed comparative to describe that which was superlative, absolutely. Nothing this side the bottomless pit, I am convinced, is quite as black as the magnificent dog that trotted over to Thorplay and looked inquiringly up into his face.

"Where's your manners?" said the man to the dog in mock severity; and the big Gordon left his master and walked over to me, to offer me the hospitality of his house.

He sniffed at me politely; then turned on me those soft, dark-hazel setter eyes through which there shines the evidence of a comradely, quiet understanding of mankind which is perhaps unequalled in the doggy world.

"Good evening," I said, making no move to touch him.

At which he switched a superb short-feathered flag, and very sedately offered me his paw.

"It's him?" I asked, as much incredulous as I was ungrammatical.

"Yousezzer!" Dan Thorplay answered, proud as an old cock pheasant.

I took a look deep into those hazel eyes as I held the setter's heavy forearm in my hand.

"But you don't mean to tell me, man, that a dog with a flame like that in his eye is gun-shy!"

"He isn't death or hell shy, that dog. Watch this," said Dan in answer. "Fetch the spike collar, Devil!"

And big Red Feather, U.S.K.A. 345726, pet-named The Devil by those who knew him, laid bare his fangs and rumbled a deadly growl. No fear was in it; only hate. But without a moment's hesitation he went over to his master's gun cabinet, and nosing into a partly open drawer below the racks picked out one of those efficient training devices which are so perfectly harmless in the hands of gentle men, but which had, not long since, in murderous hands, tortured him close to the brink of a miserable and abject end. All the while muttering to himself, he dragged the steel-barbed collar forth and delivered the detested thing into his master's hand. Then, much to my amazement and delight, for I am little used to flattery, he came back to me and sat down between my feet. I could feel his throat cords still vibrating silently when I stroked his neck.

"How'd you like to put that collar on him?" Thorplay asked me.

"If it's all the same to you, and you think you'd enjoy the performance just as much, I believe I'd rather put it on a cheetah."

With that wonderful long silk head in my hands I settled back into my seat again.

"As I hinted before," I said to Thorplay, "I hold all the indoor listening records from ten minutes to all night; and I'm specially good on dog stuff. I asked you once before what you did about that last little billet-doux from friend M. Arrendale. You go from there."

"Well, first of all," my host took up his story, "I ripped that twenty-five-hundred-dollar check to confetti. That took a great load off my chest. Then I made out a new one. I wrote in the amount myself— double the figure that I knew was right. I looked about for a little sheet of asbestos after that, but couldn't find a bit; so I risked the few remarks I had to make to Arrendale on a piece of ordinary writing paper and kept my eye on it a minute. My grip on the English language must have been weak that day, for the paper didn't even scorch, so I folded it up in disgust and stuck it in an envelope together with the newly written check. I was about to seal it when I recalled that Arrendale's letter had said, 'When the check's returned the setter is yours'; so I dumped the confetti into the envelope, too, closed it, and mailed the whole mess to Ohio—and kept the dog. Was that all right?"

"What could be fairer?" I replied, running a broad, thin, gold-lined ear between my fingers. "You couldn't send him back."

"You're dad-whanged whistling I couldn't send him back!" Dan detonated; his adverbs, though, as I recall them, being somewhat different than here recorded. "But that new check never was cashed, and it's been out about six months now."

"Oh, well," I ventured a cheerful prophecy, "he's like most wealthy men; he's busy; and doubtless he's been waiting just such a business let-down like the present one to give him the leisure to make a few friendly calls. He'll be dropping in to see you one of these days."

Dan Thorplay is a little man. But you'd be surprised at the size of the implement of warfare that replaces his hand when he gathers up his various knuckles and bunches them all together.

"Do you honestly think that?" asked Dan. "That's

just the very thing I've been afraid of all the time."
And he evidenced his craven dread of such an event by
the pensive faraway look that comes into his blue eyes
on occasion.

It dawned on me as Dan sat there, wistfully regarding that mean eight-cornered fist of his, that it was only
a step from the present stage of our jaw-fest to the
late Franco-American affair at Boyle's plot of ground,
and to the gentle art of knuckle shoving in general.
And though I realize that this is a thing that must
come up eventually wherever two or more men are
gathered together, yet I am a firm believer in one thing
at a time—and that dogs come first; so I switched
Dan's thoughts into less carnal channels by asking
him how he worked on a gun-shy pupil.

"In the first place," Dan informed me as that lethal
instrument on the end of his tanned forearm opened
up and metamorphosed into a human hand again,
"you don't dare punish a dog for that. He's scared
enough when you start. Kindness, patience and
hunger form the basis of every dog trainer's method.
It's simple enough. You lay the gun beside the dog's
dinner pan. If he doesn't come out of his kennel and
eat you take the gun away—and his dinner with it.
Then you show him neither gun nor grub for twenty-
four hours—and repeat. Meanwhile treat him fine.
He'll not last long. Then use the same medicine so
that he lets you handle the gun while he eats; and the
same dose again till he lets you fire over him. I've
seen dogs stick it out five days when it comes to shoot-

ing. But he finally starts to eat in spite of the report; and when he does, good evening. You couldn't scare him away from that long-lost grub pile with a dreadnought's broadside; and he's cured. The method is infallible. At least we thought it was until we tried it on Red Feather.

"I'd give something to know what hideous abuse a dog could suffer and still live, to make him as gunshy as that Gordon was. We never got past the first stage with him. He fasted seven days, first crack, with the steam of hot beef rump in his very nose, just because an old shotgun lay in the dust beside his dinner pan. On the eighth day I surrendered and took away the gun. I thought he'd eat the dish. We fed him up a little and made another try. This time it took him nine days to make me quit. He was so weak we almost lost him that time. Then in desperation, we tried it with his water bowl; but he beat me in two days with that. I couldn't stand it. I was done. Licked. I gave him up.

"And all the while there was growing this mighty love affair between the dog and my youngster. The kid's first shout in the morning was a masterful attempt to say the dog's name. But far as he came from getting it right, his burble never had to be repeated. The setter slept by the kid's door, and his eager yap of greeting was the thing that told us every morning that the king was awake and demanding his bodyguard, and that the dog was asking immediate entrance to the throne room. All day long the pair would be together, and night would find the Gordon sleeping at the baby's door again. Andy MacAndrews christened the combination Ham and Eggs.

"If it hadn't been for this mighty attachment I would have shot the dog myself, for he was utterly worthless, and I had begun to think that it was really the alleged Gordon yellow, after all, that was the trouble with him. The paralysis from the cruel abuse of the spiked collar had entirely disappeared, and as he grew strong and sleek the memory of his pitiable condition when he reached us faded. I began to doubt if such a man ever lived who could treat a dog badly enough to make of him the arrant, hopeless coward that Red Feather was. He must be just naturally yellow. Roosters chased him. Gophers scared him silly. And when a jack jumped out in front of him he'd tuck in his tail and never stop till safe in his kennel; or better still, till he reached the sanctuary which he seemed to think surrounded him when he put his head into the chubby arms of my kid.

"And then the miracle. One day as I sat at this table here I became aware that a very dreadful voice was calling to me quietly from the porch. It was Madge's—Mrs. Thorplay's—voice, the tone very low and soft. But the agony! My flesh moved cold and prickly under my skin as I sat, frozen stiff, and listened.

" 'Bring a gun! Bring a gun! Bring a gun,' she was saying over and over again in a dead, terrible undertone, 'Bring a gun! Bring a gun! Bring a gun!'

"Icy with dread, I took the forty-five out of the desk and tiptoed to the porch. Madge was standing rigid, with her hand against a pillar. Her face was ghastly grey. Her eyes filled full with a torture that tore at the pillars of her reason. For the bright sun-drenched air in the yard beyond her was filled with a dry and wicked rustling such as, once heard, no man will ever mistake should he live ten thousand years.

"The boy was down on his hands and knees, crawling to reach the beautiful rattling toy. And not a yard away, that deadly sportsman who warns the world that all he wants is to be left alone, raised his flat head above the shining, black-diamonded yellow coils that the baby wanted, and buzzed his hideous threat.

"I tried to level my gun, but a palsy of terror and fear had turned my muscles to rags. Then I felt my wife's hand on my arm, and somehow some of the strength flowed out of her slim body into my own; for suddenly I became aware that I was looking down steadily over the long revolver barrel. I waited; and after a thousand years I saw the frightful, wide-open jaws, with the hinged fangs already thrown down, swing back under my gun sights. I twitched a numb finger. Powder roared. A spurt of dust leaped high behind the diamond-back. And before I realized that I had missed, the girl beside me sprang like some tigress mother for the space between the baby and the snake. The flat head struck."

Dan Thorplay drew a handkerchief from his pocket. I'll venture the drops that glistened on his brow at the mere recital of that horror were clammy and cold. He mopped the moisture off while I sat in silence and ran that silken ear between my fingers. Then slowly, as I waited for him to go on, I became aware that he was waiting for me to climax his story. Somehow my eyes drew involuntarily down to the glorious head on my thigh. I looked deep into the gentle, fearless hazel eyes of Red Feather, pet-named The Devil; and suddenly it dawned.

"The dog!" I almost shouted.

"The dog," repeated Dan Thorplay quietly.

I bent and laid my face very reverently against that wonderful muzzle.

"You came through, old fire eater," I whispered. "You came through, for the love of the kid." And the cold nose nuzzled along my ear.

"Came through?" Dan fairly snorted. "Did he come through? I'm here to inform the United States of America that I'm the only living man who ever saw a black lightning flash. If you and me can come through like that when old Charley Bones with the scythe and lipless grin beckons us with a skeleton finger, we're men! There isn't a breathing animal, Church, domestic or wild, that doesn't know exactly who the grim spectre is that backs up a diamond-back's buzz. Yet the dog who would cringe when a lark got up in under his nose was whirling hell-bent right into that devil's bell when my forty-five went off in his face. And the dog that would run himself sick at the snap of a boy's cap pistol snarled his contempt at that

big gun's bark, and closed his teeth on the rattler's spine
when its fangs were less than an inch from the baby's
laughing face.

"You never saw such a mix-up. Seven feet of snake
and a hundred pounds of dog in the wildest tangle of
flesh and blood and dust and death that ever tore up
the earth. Madge snatched up the kid and leaped for
the porch; and I, with the fear that the snake might
escape and crawl under the house, yelled for a club,
and, no one putting a club in my hand, stood over the
gun-shyest dog between two oceans and emptied the
other five chambers of the forty-five into that snarling
and hissing mess.

"Escape and crawl under the house? Fat chance!
The berserk rage that gave The Devil his proper title
around this dump never died out till that seven-foot
snake was torn into bits the size of your hand. There
was never a deader snake, nor a prouder pup. Lucky
to tell, my marksmanship that day was my worst exhibition in years of atrocious gunnery; for except for
a bit of hair clipped off one shoulder, and a groove
gouged out along The Devil's ribs, I hadn't made a
single score in six times up.

"He staggered over toward us after he had finished
his job on the rattler, stopped on the way and swayed
as the venom laid its finger on his heart, shook his head
for all the world like a fighter who tries to fling off the
dizziness of a knockout punch. The in-closing mists
must have cleared for a moment; for with head and
tail high he came tottering bravely over to where we

stood at the foot of the steps.   He took a contemptuous
sniff of the smoking gun I still held in my hand and
reared up with his front paws on his mistress' shoulders.   He tried with a weakly lolling tongue to reach
the baby's hands, but as the kid bent and stretched out
his fat fingers the vertigo struck, and the heavy dog
slipped down through my best girl's arms, fell on his
side and commenced to swell."

And so Dan Thorplay, being a better story-teller
than most, would have ended his narrative.   But I
couldn't see it.   The vacant space between that pitiful
venom-puffed dog and the animal under my hands
yawned like a gulf before me.

So I said, "Well?"

And Dan Thorplay took me to task.   "See here,"
he said, "if you're ever going to get this yarn past an
editor's desk you'll have to leave a little something to
the imagination.   Every good story does that.   I guess
you're sore at Rembrandt for not getting out a detail
sheet of the rivets in the Golden Helmet."

But I've got a skin that's proof against heavier shot
than that; so I simply repeated my monosyllable.
And after a little silence, broken by the musical clink-
ing of ice in glass, he capitulated.

"I found the punctures while Mrs. Thorplay was getting the whisky," he went on as he put the tall tumbler
down.   "Luckily they were on a foreleg, where a
twisted handkerchief was just about as effective as a
surgeon's elastic tourniquet would have been.   So I
shut off the blood on the heart side of the oozy holes,

and ripped out the meat for a couple square feet around with my pocketknife. Then the girl held his head on her lap and opened the pouch of his lips and I poured enough good liquor between his teeth to plaster a mule. After which I got Doc Holden on long distance and talked with him while Mrs. Thorplay sat on the floor in a corner with the boy to her breast and prayed. If you want any more details I'll give you a letter of introduction to Doc. He likes a good listener better than I do. And he left the best veterinary practice on his side of the Mississippi go to thunder for a month to stick with The Devil. Personally, I have my doubts if it should have taken as long as that to work out the poison and to fix up the terrible mess I'd made of the poor pup's leg; but it happened that there were about fifty million prairie chickens in Texas about that time, and Doc had the idea that they all required his personal attention.

"Of course the thing that interested us above all other things in regard to Red Feather's recovery was whether the little spark of courage that this beast Arrendale had failed to quench would continue to blaze as it had at sight of the baby's peril.

"We found out. The dog hadn't been on his feet a week when he went the rounds of the kennels. It appears that he had some overdue accounts that demanded settlement there. All innocent of the knowledge that here was no yellow-spined mutt, but the devil himself, the first dog he met rushed forth and sailed into him. The rest he had to catch. Some new dogs had arrived during his convalescence, and they, of course, had never had the opportunity to take a crack at the village coward; but just to avoid the semblance of showing any partiality whatsoever, old Beelzebub went from one kennel run to the other and systematically walloped the dog-gone whey out of every dog on the place. Want to see how gun-shy he is?" ended Dan.

He stuck the handle of a long blue service revolver into my hand.

"Take a chance at the top log there," he directed, nodding his head toward the fireplace.

I looked at him a little amazed, I guess.

" 'Sall right," he said, with a sort of carte-blanche wave of the hand. "This place has been Bachelor's Hall for the last two months. The lady has had her young son up North, in New York, visiting Grandpop & Co. She's due back here tomorrow, the Lord be praised for all his tender mercies and loving-kindnesses. But if we feel like holding forty-five target practice in our living room—we do it, by heck! That's the kind of ruffians we are—till tomorrow."

I aimed at the log and actually hit it. The embers and charcoal flew, and with a cloud of sparks the burning chunk jumped out of its place and clattered down out of sight in the back of the hearth. And the rafters rang and rang again.

"Dead-Eye Pete!" yelled Dan in noisy approval.

But the long black-and-gold muzzle on my thigh raised very deliberately, and the soft ears went forward in polite and calm inquiry. A setter, however, talks with his eyes. Any bird-dog man will tell you that. The Devil turned up to me two deep unfathomable hazel wells, with tiny twin sparks of Cerberus-red aglow way down in the darkness.

"Say, mister," those fine eyes asked, "where in hell do you keep your rattlesnakes?"

There's another chapter. Dan's story is done. But next day there happened such an absolutely delectable thing that a man could be sent to the chair for keeping it under his hat. If you say you'll stick we'll give the old rhetoric wrecker another gallon of heavy and see what we can get out of her concerning that luscious twenty-five minutes.

Tired out by what amounts to almost a continental trip across the never-ending state of Texas, I slept soundly and late next day; but at last there reached down into the hay where I lay comatose an insulting series of blares from an auto horn. I stretched a furlong or two, and rose and went to the window. The biggest and dustiest touring car in the world was standing in the front yard, raucously demanding the immediate attention of whatever menials happened to inhabit this place where it had deigned to stop.

Dan's ancient smoke came scuffling out to the dreadnought, and the snarling horn subsided a moment.

"Yassah!" said Ephraim Terwilliger Joppey. "Yassuh! Boss he say, please, sah, quiet dat snorter a li'l' Boss got a li'l' settah bitch hadn't orter be 'stuhbed no moh'n kin be he'ped. Done had a ve'y bad houh, dat li'l' settah, and' de boss won' leave huh nohow now till de las' pup's done whelped. Will you set on de po'ch an' wait?"

A surly refusal had the effect of sending the darky around the house in the direction of the kennels, muttering to himself.

Then a squeaky voice from the back of the car said, "Sit on that button, Josephs, till we see if we can't get somebody out of that dump besides a nigger to talk to."

Josephs evidently sat; for the blaring broke out again and kept it up without a break while I scrambled into my clothes so as to be downstairs on the scene when the storm struck.

I had reached the veranda, and was stepping down to cross the yard in order to do what I could to calm that impatient bellowing, when I saw Dan steaming toward the car from the other side. The visitors were looking toward me and didn't see Dan; and the siren was still insultingly blowing when Thorplay stepped up and without a word lifted the hood and jerked loose the wires that led to the bawling instrument's motor.

"My own wood burner gets its horn button stuck like that sometimes," said Dan in the sudden silence. He was addressing the occupant of the back seat and ignoring the chauffeur's windy protestations. "But you're bound to have more or less trouble with the cheaper cars, aren't you, Mr. Arrendale?"

I put up my ears like a mule.

"I'm Arrendale; but damned if I know how you guessed it," said that absurdly high and ratlike voice.

And the door flew out and a little foot on the end of a monstrous, sausage balloon of a leg reached down for the running board. I had pictured this Arrendale tall, and spare, and bearded, and cruel, and dark. Like the old grandees. Like Alva. But instead, there rolled out on the running board, and thence to the ground, the roundest-faced, fairest-faced, grossest, most bestial, ferret-eyed, slimy seacow of a man that ever rod leather.

"There was no need of guessing it," Dan explained obligingly. "Doc Holden told me what you looked like. We almost came to blows about it. I told him he wasn't describing a man, but a grampus. And here we were both right all the time!"

The roses and cream in Mr. Arrendale's pudgy face turned purple, and a couple of half-choked squeaks came out of his throat. He clenched a small white fist.

Dan turned to me like a flash.

"You saw him threaten me, didn't you, Church?" he demanded.

But my skull was too thick. I didn't get it. So I stood speechless, like some doddering nitwit, waiting for the light to break.

Just then MacAndrews came up.

"Threaten you, boss?" says Andy. "I saw him wallop you; the big fat stiff—to be picking on a little fellow like you!"

"It's a matter of pure self-preservation.   I've simply got to sock him, Church," Dan explained.   "You saw him assault me, yourself, didn't you?"

And the great light dawned.

"Most assuredly, kind sir," I spoke up.   "It must have been aggravating.   Especially so when he kicked you in the mush when he had you down!"

"And now," said Dan, turning to the blotch on the landscape, "you see how it is.   I am forced to defend myself against you.   With these reputable witnessess on my side, there's not a Texas jury from Jackson County to Dallam that wouldn't acquit me of a charge of assault.   So prepare yourself, dog butcher, for a body beating that will leave its mark on every one of your great-grandchildren!"

And while I stood and gloated, Dan Thorplay unbuckled his hardware and dropped it at his feet.   Dan shouldn't have done it.   Dan is a six-gun toter, and a dead shot.   But get us right, for the love of Pete.   It isn't a Tom Mix Texas where this came off.   But ever since Dan missed that snake three feet in front of his boy he's practised shooting till he can knock the eye brows off a gnat at twenty-five feet and never scratch its face.   And he goes about loaded for rattlers all the time; the only man left in the Lone Star State with a gun on his thigh.   And, of course, at the very thought of a fight the first thing he did was to get rid of the shooting iron, to give him freer action for other weapons.   But the minute that forty-five hit the dust

I saw a dirty cunning look steal into the pig face over beside the car.

Dan rolled up his sleeves and advanced a stride, that faraway sad look casting a pensive shadow over his face. And Arrendale went back a quaking stealthy step; reached backward into the car, and a second later was sighting a malignant boar's eye down between the two barrels of a shotgun that was pointing fair at the pit of Dan Thorplay's stomach.

"I brought this along to kill that yellow-backed cur of mine," squeaked the absurd little voice. "He's my dog, and I'll shoot him to death and to hell with how much your slobbery brat may love him. This gun isn't loaded for birds; it's loaded for mutts—and that lets you in. And that self-defence game can be played two ways. I'd pull this trigger as quick as you'd use your fists. Where's my setter, you damned little shrimp?"

When I picture that wonderful Thorplay kid, who came home that very same night, bringing along with him a star-eyed girl whom Dan called mother, but who would have blocked the traffic for several miles each way if she had ever ventured to cross Broadway at forty-second in the present-day style of skirt, I shudder to think of what might have happened. But just as the tension reached the point where something was due to snap, the answer to Arrendale's question, in the life, came bounding around the end of the house. Red Feather himself! He took a leap or two toward the

familiar figures of Dan and Andy; and a swinish look
of pleasure came over Arrendale's face as he swung
the gun on the dog.

Dan crouched to spring.

A voice from the driver's seat in the big car said,
"Careful there!"

My heart went sick as I saw the shining thing that
gave weight to the chauffeur's warning.

Unaware of his doom the big black setter came leaping on; and then, sudden and unexpected as lightning
out of a bright noon sky, there happened the thing
that prevented at least two unarmed men from taking
a sportsman's chance at sudden death.

Fair in the midst of a bound, with all four feet in
the air, the setter went stiff; and the plump, white
disgustingly tapered finger that had actually started to
press the trigger to blast that splendid and shining
creature to a mangled smear of bloody meat went
slack in amazement.

Red Feather hit earth half statue. A moment his
nose searched the breeze, head high. With infinite
caution, as though close on a covey of quail
the magnificent neck curved slowly away from
us. One forefoot lifted. The tail grew straight and
still. The whole form sank ever so little, crouching
and then, with his long black muzzle thrust straight
at Arrendale, the setter froze to a glorious point.

A breeze blew past us and waved the fringe on his
tail and the golden feather on his legs. Then the warm
zephyr died, and the midday sun, in dazzling arrow

"—and then, with his long muzzle thrust straight at Arrendale, the setter froze to a glorious point."

of pure black light, came blazing off of a marble dog, done from a block of Italy's beautiful black and gold.

It was first surprise, and curiosity next, that kept Arrendale's gun from spraying that wonderful sculpture with whistling lead. What setter had ever pointed a man before? The fat man stood and squinted over his gun with a puzzled look on his face; and as he stood, the baby-pink colour slowly faded out of his plump, smooth cheeks and left them pasty and grey. For there, before his eyes, all the old fallacies regarding the setter's stand were being laid forever to rest. No catalepsis there; no modified drop to the ancient fowler's net; no instinctive location of game for the benefit of man, the superior god.

The fingent hands of man! He has caught this eager pose and moulded the dog's intensest moment in life to his own desires; has taught him to hold in abeyance the keen hunting lust that Nature has planted in every nerve tendril and every blood drop of him at the very point where the saliva is hot in his jaws and the chance to leap and kill has tautened his muscles to steel.

There was no mistaking the thing. The eagerly twitching nose; the forward-stretched head; the caution; the forepaw raised, to take one nearer step in order to make more sure the final spring, provided that all-wise nose said that another step might be taken without putting the quarry to flight; and the eyes, the glowing and savage eyes, wild with the hunter's passion to seize and kill. All these told the five of us standing there one thing: The Devil had scented his prey!

Hate and murderous rage surged hot through the big black dog as the breeze brought up to his nostrils the loathsome, familiar scent. Fear was gone, swept away long since and destroyed for ever in that wild whirl at venomous horrible death for the love of a little boy. Death glared at him again, out of the two dark, close-set, bright-rimmed eyes of that shotgun's barrels, and no one knew it better than the dog. Yet The Devil, with infinite caution, put down the upheld forepaw, a little ahead of its mate, and let his whole gleaming body stretch forward another inch.

"Steady!"

No field-trial setter, that stiffened again at his master's warning voice. No slim Llewellyn, built for speed and range. No pointer, clean-limbed and elegant, with the limitless hound endurance of his long-lost forbears showing in every thoroughbred line. No Irish setter, of grace and sheer symmetry passing the words of men.

A Gordon; despised by many, admired by few; but a dog among dogs, for all that. Bred for conditions the bird dog must seldom meet. Big, heavy, mighty of substance and bone, flat-coated; bold-eyed and stubborn-willed, to match, perhaps, the splendid faults of the men of his native heaths. Moulded a hundred years ago by the Dukes of Gordon to work through savage Scotch weather the punishing country and stubborn cover of the wild Caledonian uplands.

Into my mind, as the black dog pointed his monstrous game, there stole the old Gordon tradition of the bloodhound cross. I had heard old bird men speak of it many a time in regard to the black setter's unmatchable work at trailing birds by foot scent when the wind was wrong to carry the body smell.

I had seen on the dog himself the heavy flew and the hint at dewlap and haw. And now—here before our eyes—was a setter keen on the man scent.

Something of the hunted culprit's unreasoning fear for the gentle trailing hounds with the grisly name must have reached the heart of Arrendale, too, for as we watched him his gun barrel wavered and the putty-grey in his baby cheeks went to chalk.

"You fat pot hunter!" came Thorplay's voice. "You never shot at a thing in your life where it made any difference whether you missed it or not. But you're not butchering little Bobwhite this time, and God help your throat if you miss!"

But The Devil was safe. Dan knew it. So did we all.

Given a two-barreled gun and a trunkful of shells and that baby-faced monster would massacre birds all day, leaving the quail beyond his limit to rot on the ground. But here he was hunted, not hunting; and with his own blobby body in jeopardy he hadn't the nerve to send his cowardly buckshot at a target that was absolutely impossible to miss.

He stood, with his gun on The Devil, and quaked like the horrid quagmire of flesh that he was, and I hope that the spirits of thousands of murdered birds rejoiced with us in the sight.

MacAndrews spoke. "I'd let him flush," he said to his boss.

Terror spread over the blubber heap's face at the words.

"No, no! No, no!" he squeaked, and his shotgun slipped from his plump white hands.

A little twig touched the trigger and the charge let go with a roar. The spraying lead tore whistling along the earth close beside the standing dog.

"Steady!" said Thorplay. "That's a fine fellow!" MacAndrews' eyes were popping.

"Did you ask is he steady to shot?" he whispered to me. But I was watching the pudding bag.

"No, no! No, no!" he continued to pipe in his thin rat voice. "Don't order him on! Don't order him on!"

The yellow heart inside that mountain of smoking tallow was icy with dread. Suddenly he whirled, and without an attempt to retrieve his gun he plunged for his car like a frightened hippo. The door was open. Doubtless he had his trouble in squeezing through it in any case. But he stumbled and fell as he tried to lift his absurdly small feet quickly and he lunged head first through the open door, and his soft paunch wedged and stuck. He struggled and kicked; but Josephs, feeling the sag of the springs, never turned to look. In his haste to be gone he tramped open his cut-out, raced his motor and, setting his lever in high, let the clutch take hold; and without the delay of gear shifting the powerful car kicked up a typhoon of dust, roared a wild adieu and was gone.

We watched. Two minutes we watched. Then, two miles down the road, the dirt cloud hid from our sight the seat of a pair of trousers, expansive beyond the dreams of a tailor's avarice, and of breadth and depth to fill with joy the heart of a bill poster. How far our friend Josephs would drive without looking back we could not know; but we did know that every jounce of the car would wedge those pulpy sides tighter around the doorway's sharp edges. And, thinking of all the pulleys and jacks and cold cutters and wedges and various other tackle that would have to be employed in the final extraction, our hearts were at peace.

"That blessed pup!" said Dan at last.

We turned and looked, and saw that the fiery black statue was still in place, his eyes on the dust screen far down the road, the crouch to leap for his prey still frozen stiff for the use of the man he loved, whatever that use might be.

"Steady to shot and steady to wing," quoth Andy.

And at thought of that wildly beating pair of blood-pudding legs, fast at one end to their far-flung acreage of breeches seat like twin blimps tethered in the wind to some broad landing field, we clung to each other and wept again.

"Come here, you devil," said Dan.

The black-and-gold marble of Italy turned to flesh and blood and galloped over to us. No doubt there

was much disappointment in the heart that hammered
beneath that glossy hide, due to the fact that the
master had flushed but had failed to kill over that
wonderful find and point. But an arm clamped tight
to the point of pain about a fellow's ribs will assuage
most any frustration.

Andy MacAndrews stooped down and rubbed The
Devil's mighty hind quarters, and then walked over
and picked up the beautiful piece that side meat had
left behind for us to remember him by.

"Little Lord Fauntleroy seemed a trifle gun-shy,"
Andy remarked as he examined the elegant stock with
a critical eye.

"Quit licking my face," scolded Dan, and took his
arm from around the setter's big barrel. Then he
grasped the dog by both cheeks and held him away
and looked him in the eye, while The Devil struggled
and growled most ferociously, meantime meeting considerable success in his attempt to wag from the tip
of his tail to the base of his skull.

"I'd say our little playmate was dog-shy too," added
Dan, glancing up from The Devil's face to mine.

I looked for the hundredth time in less than twenty-
four hours at the puzzling boy-blue of Dan Thorplay's
eyes. As I said before, Dan's a little fellow. But
they don't have to come so big when they assay one
hundred and ten per cent male.

"Old college chum, Count Firkin, seemed just the
least bit man-shy too," I ventured my own opinion.

MacRonan

A placard like that was tacked to the back of the giant dog's clean stall. A mouthful of elegant words, those last. Dripping honey. Smelling a little of raw bear meat. Balm to the soul. Man-talk! If you didn't get it at first, ssh! then, and cock an ear over this way. "He very seldom fights;—but when he does—" Nice?

He looked it. Two hundred pounds of him I judged. Two hundred pounds as he lay stretched out lazily there and blinked a dark eye while he let the world and the dog-show wag. His fighting weight? That's different! Now you're asking something. I put to myself the same delectable question, and casting an appraising eye on him I found again that amber spark a-smoulder deep down inside the black and hazel well of one sleepily winking optic. A thousand pounds,

47

says I to myself. And then he yawned. Moved by a common impulse, the crowd before his bench shoved back into a respectful semi-circle; and I doubled my figure. Two thousand, I made it. Conservatively. Half a ton would be only half an estimate of the heft of him in battle who could unsheath a row of weapons such as glistened in those gaping jaws.

I turned to the girl beside me.

"But Shiela," I said, "I thought his race died out after the last wolf was killed in Ireland, a couple hundred years ago."

My sister's eyes were sparkling as she stood tip-toe and stretched her slim neck to glimpse him over the crowd.

"He did work himself out of a job, the mighty rascal," was her answer, "but his breed wasn't allowed to die—small glory to the Irish. An Englishman it was who made a breath-snatching rescue of him at the very brink of extinction."

An Englishman? And yet who else? Lay your tongue to the English, and if it isn't me, it'll be some other short nosed lad you'll find listening to you with the smile of angels on his face. But this you'll have to say, before you're finished, if you're giving the devil his due at the time; that no race has produced a sportsman the like of him, nor a lover of dogs to approach him at all;—much as it troubles my soul to admit it, for I'd have a job for myself thinking a kinder word to say for the very saints.

"The name he has!" whispered Shiela. "Take it

between your teeth now, Pat, and get the feel of it
against the roof of your mouth. Whist, while I say it
for you." And she said it. And when she chooses,
this Shiela Malloy can set her slim throat and her wide
red mouth to a glorious brogue. A thing to inherit,
not to acquire; the real Irish brogue; a thing not to
be put on paper, nor to be heard over vaudeville foot-
lights. More a matter of richness, huskiness, mellow-
ness, than of pronunciation; more as though each word
was held in the mouth as long as might be before it
was let go, and then let go with a sort of caress; with
soft breath soughing through it, making it fill up the
whole mouth cavity. It's a gift of the sod. The
speech of aged Irishmen has it. On this side the
young generation possesses it rarely. Women have it
almost never. 'Twas so her mother's voice was, our
dad would always be telling us. Saints aid the man on
whom that Shiela chooses to use it. He's entirely
lost. Silver of flute shot through with the gold of
clarinet reeds.

"Keelta MacRonan!"

A soft arpeggio plucked from the strings of an
Irish harp would make no better music. And I had
been thinking that next to being American, I was
Irish, because my name was Pat Aloysius Malloy!

It's a love sigh; Keelta MacRonan! It's a battle
yell; Keelta MacRonan! It's a conjure word; try
it. Whisper it, and a lute sings. Roar it, and a war
trumpet blares. Make magic with it, and the tangled
shores of a rain-whipped Irish lake stretch away

before you. The call of horns comes ringing out of the copse. Danger lays bare pointed teeth in a red-lipped, inviting grin. 'Ware you! The white tusked wild hog makes his rush out of such brakes as these! Up on the side of that emerald hill hoarse music like the clangour of iron bells tells where the hounds are at work. A bellow! The stag's at bay! The big broth kettles will moisten the rafters with savoury steam tonight. Meat will be bubbling on every spit. Not bleating meat. Not lowing, squealing meat; dragged up, shoved in, knocked down, gullet slit by besmeared mechanics in some blood-fouled slaughter hole; but meat with the tangle of copse about it in which to try it's cunning—meat with the whole of pristine Ireland before it in which to try its speed! Meat with a chance! And if death at last, then death in the open, under the sky—in a fight! A finer end for deer, or boar—or man? You name it.

Keelta MacRonan! Wolfdog! Conjure words, both—to set a man a-dreaming.

How many people tried the music of that great hound's name on their tongues cannot be told; but the total attendance figures for the three days he graced Madison Square Garden with his majestic presence would not miss it much. The desire to hear it, after seeing it in print was almost irresistible. While we were standing at his bench a dozen people said it, I believe, and said it well, for it nearly pronounces itself. But MacRonan's response to the endless repetitions of his name was the languid holding open of one pair of lids from time to time, just long enough to let a brown-black eye search through the crowd before him in hope of locating master of kennel-man. But soon, while his name was being spoken, like as not, the dark fire would be veiled, as he abandoned himself to the endless tedium that was, to him, syonymous with dog-show. Timid hands reached hesitatingly forward once in a while to touch his flank. Bolder ones rubbed his whiskered muzzle now and then. Not a stir in the great neck muscles that would have lifted his head. Not the flicker of a finely folded ear.

Then, thump—thump—thump! Straw was disturbed on his bench almost a yard behind him, and the thin boards beneath him rattled as though from mallet blows under the thrash of the great tail. I looked about. The group before him was still drawn back in the arc that had formed at the start of his cavernous, whitefanged yawn. No sign of any one approaching either way who might have stirred that long flail into action. I searched the aisle again. No one who fitted in with that contented thumping. MacRonan's eyes were merest slits. His nose would tell him little, for the giant Irishman is a sight hound. His ears then—they must have caught some message.

I had it!

"Shiela," I said, "you're the first one who's said it right! That little 'q' sound in the 'k' gets to him. He likes it."

As pleased a smile as ever turned up the corners of that bewildering mouth of hers flashed up at me.

"No blarney, now. You really think that?" she asked. And at my nod she slipped her hand in the crook of my arm.

"Let's try it again, close range," she said, and dragged me toward the bench.

"Hello, Big Fellow!" said I, tentatively, crowding a little in front of Shiela, so as to be between her and the monstrous dog, "How's things?"

The tip of the Big Fellow's thick rooted tail came down on the boards with one last thump; for all the world like a dropped rope end; and the straw back him was still. It seemed that it was no affair of mine how things was.

I tried again. "A gentleman registered under so long a name would surely have a shorter one around the kennels. A pet name that might get a wag or two for the man who could hit it right. 'Mac,' I should say." I stooped and laid my hand on his big shoulder. "How's that for a guess, Mac, old war-horse?"

The guess was poor, or maybe the trouble was with the guesser. At any rate the long ribs heaved a sigh of ennui, and the narrow slit of hazel-black closed altogether. That for Pat Malloy!

"One side," laughed Shiela, hugely enjoying my discomfiture. "If you don't know how to talk to regular folks, quit standing right in front of those that do."

I let her shoulder me aside; but I kept my eyes on

the hound as she formed her throat to the proper brogue.

"Keelta MacRonan!" Soft and low.

He was up! Tail swinging in a great circle. No lumbering heave of front and clumsy upsurge of the back of him. A catlike gathering of his mighty muscles and one easy lift that threw him to his full three feet at shoulders almost instantaneously. Then the long, bristling muzzle thrust out toward my sister's face. I took a step to go between the two. The long tail still was waving in its wide, full circle, reassuringly; but the savage whiskers! and the bristled brows! and the deep fire in those eyes! But Shiela pushed against me with a strong hand, and waited. Slowly the wild, ferocious muzzle, lined, as we knew, with dagger teeth, came forward. A woman back of us gave a little cry. But my own muscles had released, for I had caught the easing of the great dog's breath. Not one girl in five thousand but would have given ground before that deliberately advancing face; if not from fear, then surely to avoid the slavery caress of a wet tongue. But Shiela actually bent forward; and as the cool, black nostrils came into feathery contact with sister's dainty nose, I saw that the wolfhound was actually holding his breath, so gentle was this giant specimen of the gentlest of all dogs. And not so much as the tip of a red tongue came out. So they stood; a picture. The shaggy beast above the slender girl; literally face to face. The fierce browed eyes of the hunter and killer of wolves searching down into the eyes of the gentlest creature God had found himself able to fashion, with infinite materials at his command, and infinite craftsmanship.

I stood behind the girl, supporting her a little, and looked deep into the brown depths of those wild eyes that seemed entirely oblivious of me—dark smouldering eyes through which a soul looked, as sure as there is soul stuff in the universe, and as I looked there formed in them a picture, half misty at the first, but wholly familiar; that cleared, at last, like the vision in some mystic's crystal.

Windy nesses ahead; and beyond them the sea, where thousands and thousands of Mananan MacLir's wild horses toss their white manes in the gloom. Behind us the marshes; lonely and wide and windswept; dank with the chilling mists of Irish winter. The wild fen path has writhed away from under our feet. The Bog has wrapped his terrible fingers around our ankles. A long howl sounds out there in the spectral drift of moor fog; closer, now that the light of the stormy day is so rapidly fading. There is desperate clinging of a slim hand on one arm. With the other I grimly test the balance of a keen Irish ax. And then, 'all in a moment, we're safe! And to prove it, there comes the caress of a sigh breathing relief from peril against my throat. She too has heard it. No mistaking that silver clink.

A little wait—a rustle in the high marsh grass—and a long, bewhiskered muzzle comes thrusting through;

savage eyes eagerly blazing in a circle of bristling brows. Skolaun! dragging beneath him half of the heavy silver chain which he had snapped apart with the mighty lunge that had started him in search of us. He reached the girl in a leap, and I braced her against me as the hound reared up. So we stood a minute; my sister leaning backward heavily against me, her white hands reaching high for Skolaun's shaggy neck, her white face hidden in the deep, sleet-covered chest; shield of the giant wolfdog's forearm timbers over her; his paws against my shoulders; his head a foot above my own. A dismal chorus wailing hate and baffled hunger comes to our ears as we stand there; but this time from some safe place far back in the fens. Wolves? A contemptuous breed!

A whisper: "Pat, you monkey!"

Scant dignity in words like that, and them to be coming out of the mouth of Yseult, a Princess of ancient Connacht. It was Shiela's voice, by the powers! I looked down; and there, as sure as the world, was Shiela Malloy's black hair puffed out beneath her little turban, her wide slim shoulders back against my chest; my arm about her. I looked about; and Ballycoordin Bog was gone. The Garden's dingy galleries soared about me, and two or three dozen people, all interest in the dog-show lost, stood in our aisle, grinning at us that tolerant and envious grin which the world bestows on brides and grooms wherever they may happen to be discovered.

I let her loose. I'm telling you, 'twill be a task to

find some other fellow's sister with a waist as supple.
I'm working at that now. As for dreams of ancient
Connacht—a man might well be dreaming. Into
my sister's eyes looked eyes in which old Irish fire
smouldered, that had been glowing there for over a
thousand years. Jaws that could crush the vertebrae
of a full grown wolf were still poised over her face.
One single snap! But as I watched; the hound's dark
eyes still searching steadily into the blue ones, his
nose still motionless against the girl's, a long and heavy
foreleg lifted, and a foot reached out, and pawed
along Shiela's side. She caught it in her left hand
and drew back laughing from the touch of the cold,
moist nose, while she shook hands with him.

"See!" I said. "He likes that little 'q' sound in the
'k.' Besides, he's heard you call his name before!"

"Nonsense!" said Shiela. "Where?"

"On Ballycoordin bogs, in Connacht," said I chuck-
ling. She would be calling her only brother 'monkey'
if he dreamed a bit. Then let her puzzle that!

"More nonsense!" was her answer, and no puzzling
at all. "You know I've never set foot on Ireland.
And besides, the name of the hound at Ballycoordin
was Skolaun!"

I stared at her, eyes popping. Her eyes were looking from their corners up at me, the devil in them. But
her colour was gone; the scarlet mouth of her now
palest rose. A lot of sister! I'll kill the man who
doesn't treat her right—lover or husband. I haven't
watched her blooming fifteen hundred years to have

some unclean slug destroy her loveliness in nineteen twenty-one.

"It's true, then," I asked eagerly, "but for the hound the wolves had gotten you?"

"What about you; red-headed brother of mine?" she answered. "Until the woman in your care was safe, you'd have no thought of your own living bones ripped bare, and your own clean meat, still quivering, bolted down fifty wolf gullets, would you?"

"What Irishman would?" I questioned.

"What American would?" was her reply.

I found her eyes at that. She was grinning a nineteen twenty-one grin at me; wide and sparkling; and the scarlet had come back.

"Pat!" she said reproachfully, "You monkey!"

"But his name—in the old days—Skolaun? How did you know it?"

"When you dream, you talk in your sleep, you big spalpeen!" she laughed, and gave me a good stiff jog in the short ribs with as firm an elbow as I care to be target for.

Then she took hold of the wolfdog's great forearm in her two hands and laid it on her shoulder.

"Quit looking into my eyes like that, big dog," she whispered. "It gives me creeps."

"No wonder," I said to her. "Nobody ever looked backward fifteen hundred years into your eyes before. Wait till some man does that. You ain't felt no creeps yet!"

She put the hound's leg down and turned to answer

me; but this, it seemed, was not the proper arrangement. That mighty timber lifted out and up, and searched for its former resting place on Shiela's shoulder, while the head lowered toward her hand with an arching of the powerful neck that would have rivalled the grace of an African barb. Attention: that's what MacRonan wanted. So Shiela took his head between her hands and pulled it down against her side, crooked an arm and forearm about it, and thrust her fingers into the defensive armour of hard hair that covered his neck. This, he would have us understand, was the proper way for a girl to talk to a red-headed man. As long as Shiela's finger-tips wandered about through the dense coat, so long it was granted that she might talk to me uninterruptedly; but let her hand forget its motion for a moment, and a nuzzling of that head beneath her arm would almost lift her from the floor. It took about a minute of this kind of love-making to bring the question I was waiting to hear.

"I wonder," said Shiela, looking up at me wistfully, her cheek against the great dog's neck, "would anybody sell a thing like this."

> "You wonder what the wolfhound breeder buys,
> One-half so precious as the goods he sells?"

A very pleasant voice said that, making its own pleasant alterations to Omar. We turned and saw a very pleasant face—a horn-rimmed-spectacled face, smiling and scholarly, topping spare, wiry shoulders. Not exactly the face of Finn MacCool. Sketch for yourself this leader of Cormac MacArt's wild Fenian militia; this master of the royal war-kennel of three hundred terrible wolfdogs, every last one of them able to run down a wolf and kill him single-handed—a thing no other living creature on the earth can do. The world's sublimest kennel, this. Fifteen score battle-dogs, trained down, hard, ready for work; some thirty tons of living, long-fanged fight and fire; and countless whelps and puppies, and many savage-faced, sweet-eyed mothers, with duties to attend to which unfitted them temporarily for hunt or war. Perhaps the uniquest military organization of all time; unmatchable in its day for speed, mobility, strength, valour and deadliness; invaluable to the divisions of ordnance and subsistence in the War Department of a king in the ancient Irish days. And the leader of it, MacCool. Finn—Gaelic for 'fair.' Tall and blonde then; red haired and blue eyed; broad chested, quick muscled, straight mouthed; with level brows that met above the deep recess where the short nose started. But the change of MacRonan's tail motion from gentle and contented swaying to a wild lashing back and forth that threatened to knock down the wire screens at each end of his stall, proclaimed as Master of Slieve Cuilinn's hounds, a kindly gentleman of mild and thoughtful countenance and average physique, who drawled out Omar softly, instead of addressing us in crisp military phrases. His smile was very genuine, however, and a wide-flashing, eminently satisfactory performance; and the eyes behind those hornframed windows were capable, I felt sure, of that metallic glisten in the pale grey of them which is the only warning certain men give out before they let you have it.

He waited till an answering smile from Shiela gave him leave to speak again.

"There's only one thing possible to buy that's more precious than the goods we sell. That's the welfare of our breed. Mac, here, is perhaps the grandest sire in the country, but if I could be convinced, and that shouldn't be impossible" (he wasn't looking *my* direction as he talked), "that I could help Irish wolfhounds by selling him, I'd have to let him go. But I'd much rather sell a puppy, of course."

"A puppy!" Shiela said, and hugged herself.

"The wolfdog is a rare breed," he went on. "You notice Mac is the only one here. There are perhaps three dozen genuine Irish wolfhounds this side of the Atlantic. No more. So wolfdog meat," a pleasant smile of apology went with his delicate way of naming price, "is worth perhaps ten dollars a pound. If you decide you'd like to own a hound, why don't you visit my kennels and see the pups? MacRonan's at his worst on the bench, too. If you could see him course a rabbit! I sometimes think he could take the kill away from a greyhound!"

He slapped the hound affectionately on the ribs, and took possession of the heavy paw; but the wolfdog lifted his leg off of his master's forearm at once, and laid it back, gently, alongside Shiela's throat.

"I've never seen the like," said the grey-eyed man, "but this lady," he found his pocket book and extended me a pasteboard, "has certainly strengthened a tradition that clings to the breed. It is said that even to this day an Irish wolfhound will show deference to a descendant of the ancient Irish kings."

Do you think that black haired scamp would look at me? It wasn't fair; for the glance I turned on her was charged to sparking with "I-told-you-so," and she should have been sport enough to meet it. I really think she avoided it so that I wouldn't see her colour fade again. Yseult of Connacht or Shiela Malloy; what did names matter; or time or place, if the spirit of an Irish princess lived in that flat-curved body of hers? But I thought I'd better button my lip, and let MacRonan do the talking. I'd been called monkey often enough for one day. Besides, after all, there was nothing supernatural in any man's conclusion that we were Irish. For one thing, I had my hat off. I looked for traces of presumptuousness about this grey-eyed man; but his smile was too frank and engaging; and his next question was so obviously a compliment that there was no taking offence at him.

"You're Irish surely?" he said. "If I'm allowed the liberty of a guess—you and your sister."

I laughed as I returned the courtesy of a card. "American," I replied, "since hyphens have gone out of fashion. The word that used to go in front of the hyphen is easy enough—so long as the lady doesn't wear a mask," here the hard edge of a French heel bit into my instep, "but are you sure of 'sister'? Most guesses are for a more interesting relationship."

"There's little similarity in your looks, that's true," said Mr. Robert Barton of Slieve Cuilinn kennels, "but you must remember that I've been fortunate enough to get a smile from both of you. And no such pair of grins ever came from different parents."

This Mr. Robert Barton had a head on him. If ever you should want to win the good graces of Shiela Malloy, just tell her that she looks like her mother, God rest her, when she smiles.

"I've heard, of course," this man was a hound himself for following up an advantage, "that in rare instances, a man and his wife have loved each other so well that with time they have started to look a little alike; but Miss Malloy lacks many, many of the years needed to bring about resemblance by any such blessed process."

A smooth tongued master of hounds; with speech more fitted to Dermot O'Dyna who had the love-spot on his forehead, than to Finn MacCool. And Shiela answered him with a show of pearls that made him bat his eyes. Then she turned to me.

"Of course we'll come to see the puppies, won't we Pat?" she said. "When can we?"

I told her when it would suit; and the date was no sooner out of my mouth than a voice I hadn't heard for six years spoke my name in my ear.

The whole inside of me went sick. I wonder why it is that fate delights in waiting for the pleasantest moments of the game, to stack the cards and deal her filthiest hands.

I always hated Lowth. Oh, not because his folks came out of County Down; there are good Ulstermen aplenty; but because Shiela was my sister. I always hated Lowth—and feared him. Mentally and physically, the man was my superior. No doubt about it; from old football days I had been scared to death of him. He was the most spectacular player that ever wore dark red; and the most consistent—and unscrupulous. Put something in his way, and he put that something out of his way—somehow—by fair means or by foul, whichever way was easiest; but if by foul means, no official ever caught him. Few of his own teammates knew how utterly vile a game that man could play. But I knew, for he fascinated me, and I had watched him. In four years the dark red team was never penalized a yard for a foul play or a rule infringement by Lowth; for he was the mental superior of any official he ever played against. The last word means just what it says. He played against the opposing team—and the officials. Rules were simply bounds for fools, laws to be obeyed by dullwits, regulations made for his especial benefit to handicap others while he himself worked free of them. And yet he broke them as he broke men, with such subtlety that in four seasons not a penalty could be charged against him.

For four years I kept Shiela away from college; no easy job, as any undergraduate with a young, good-looking sister will attest. Sophomore Cotillon, Junior Hop, Senior Prom—all these went by year after year with Shiela chafing at the bit, at home; for the Dark-red men in our town showered her with invitations to all of them. I exhausted every wile and artifice at my command to hide my real objection from her, but finally I had to tell her that if Lowth ever met her, I'd have to kill the man.

For at each of the big annual class dances there was Lowth—looking like a god, dancing like a faun, talking like the devil, muscles of a Hercules, not half masked by the formal lines of his perfect clothes—a great, beautiful thing, into whose crawling soul only a few of us had looked. Not an important undergraduate function, but became a ghastly thing for me. For it was sure—dead sure—that the most beautiful girl who came to it would meet Lowth. Lowth would see to that. Lowth, with the deadliest arm a college base-runner ever tried to outspeed; with the mightiest bat a college pitcher ever quailed before; a two-miler who finished his last hundred in ten-three; a raging terror to every goalkeeper that ever dodged his bullet shots before a lacrosse net; a demon in moleskin. The Wilbur scholarship was tucked inside his belt. Phi Beta Kappa and Tau Beta Pi were intellectual accomplishments that faded into insignificance alongside his endless list of more desirable college honours. And Lowth could be the very gentlest of all gentlemen.

Of course he'd meet her. His judgment was unerring. His choice perfection; such a girl as is always queen of a big college dance; gay, sweet, outrageously alive, full of clean devilment, pure as starlight; by God, the thing was ghastly.

Only a couple of us knew. We always tried to get these girls away from him. But we always played according to rules, like half-wits; and, besides, what chance had any man against Denis Lowth in any game—most of all this one? And the world no more blamed or suspected him for the smirching of these lovely girls than the officials blamed him for the unconscious, broken boys that they carried away from the scrimmages that hid his dirty work. He was too clever. And the rules of decent living that hampered other men left the field clear for him. So I kept Shiela away from Valley Tech; for I didn't want to have to kill the man. Go ahead—smile. But what would you advise? My last possession would have gone down on the wager that she'd be the one girl to turn wildcat on his hands. But what good would that have done? Lowth would like that. And what Lowth liked and wanted—that he took. Once they met, there would be nothing left to do but kill him. Should I? That question never entered my head. Could I?

We graduated, and six years went by. Lowth had chosen steel; the hardest game. That's why he chose it. And in six years prodigious success had come to him. Starting without a dollar, without an ounce of pull, without family, with nothing but sheer ability, he had gone tearing over and through the opposition of the most gruelling business in the world, and had landed fair on top. I watched the rocket career of him; hating him every inch of the way; knowing that the rules that guided other men merely placed them under handicap when they met Lowth. Loyal friends felt his knife in their backs up to the hilt, and thought it was some enemy's blade, so skilfully he planned; and died their commercial deaths, still loyal to him. Rules of business decency and business morals were subtly set aside for his swift passage, and as subtly replaced again once he had passed. And yet so marvelous was the brain he used that no one ever knew that rules were broken.

And here was Lowth beside me, saying, "By this and that, if it isn't Red Malloy!" with a heartiness in his jovially affected brogue, and in his bone-cracking handshake that, I believe, would actually have disarmed me had I not caught his glance at Shiela and seen in his eye a different sort of light than brightens old classmates' faces when they meet.

He had seen her, and the damage was done; so I introduced him to Shiela and Mr. Barton.

"Not Denis Lowth!" said Shiela. Her eyes were wide as she took in the breadth of him.

"Sure, Denis Lowth!" he said. "Your brother's spoken about me, then?"

"Many's the awful thing!" she answered, and turned to me. "I always told you you were prejudiced." Her tone was bantering. "Being an Ulsterman con-

demns nobody, you big Connacht bog-trotter! Cu-
chulainn was an Ulsterman, and he stood off the whole
Connacht army single handed—and the Gailiana of
Leinster thrown in for good measure!" Her finger
wagged in exaggerated menace under my nose. But
I could plainly see the sparkle of excitement in her
eyes; and an almost imperceptible lowering of her
brows sent me the message that she was on her guard.

She looked toward Lowth again, and he turned that
grin of his loose on her. The thing's invaluable to
him, keeping in mind the game he plays. It's utterly
disarming. An honest sparkle in his eyes, a dimple
in each cheek, a broad flash of teeth, a deepening of
the long lines that flank his upper lip—even a little
wholesome chuckle to go with it—I knew it—and on
the next down the opposing captain doubled up, writh-
ing in agony on the ground when the pile of players
untangled from above him. So potent was the thing
that Shiela, knowing what she did, actually reached
out to take the hand he had extended to her at my
introduction.

"Look out!" cried Barton, and jumped forward.
There had been no motion in the straw; no scratching
of iron-clawed feet; no jerking taut of the bright
chain—but there was ample need for Barton's warning, just the same. A growl, so low and deep as to
be scarcely audible, a thing the great hound could no
more control than he could control the beating of his
heart, came to our ears. Involuntary. More than
that—irrepressible; for I know now that the Irish

wolfdog does not warn. He very seldom fights; but when the need for fighting is absolute—when the thing must be done—when there is no other way—he does not warn. No stealth nor cowardly cunning marks his attack; but he knows what all great fighters—all successful fighters—know: that the man or beast who warns an opponent that he will do thus and so to him hands his enemy a shield that is often impossible to pierce. I know now that the great hound tried to repress that warning growl! And yet it rumbled deep down in his chest, involuntarily; wild, savage and terrible; petrifying. And Denis Lowth's hand, which I am sure had never halted in anything it had ever started to do, stopped stiff, the fingers hungrily curved for grasping, the palm of it not a quarter of an inch from Shiela's palm.

Barton's quiet voice said "Mac!" That murderous snarl died away inside MacRonan's mighty chest. Lowth's palm met Shiela's in a long handclasp. I should have killed him then and there. Instead, I talked.

Shiela had seated herself on the edge of the bench and the big wolfdog had promptly lowered himself to the straw again and as promptly gone to sleep, with his head in Shiela's lap. The crowd before Mac-Ronan's bench moved on and was now exclaiming over the long line of Borzoi, MacRonan's exquisite Russian cousins, many times removed, who occupied the stalls next to him. Barton had disappeared toward one of the many dressing rooms beneath the galleries, the dog's water pan under his arm.

"Lowth," I said, "the time for acting's over. I'll lay my cards face up. I feel just like the wolfdog does about you. Leave her alone."

I've never seen so utterly contemptuous a smile.

"Do you know," he said, "I suffered the greatest disappointment of my life when you introduced that lovely creature to me as your sister."

That puzzled me. It couldn't be that my attitude would keep him away from her. But his next words cleared that point.

"I hoped she was your wife," he said.

He looked down at my clenching hands, laughed softly, turned his back insolently to me, and spoke to Shiela.

"Your brother says he shares the wolfdog's affection for me. But you? Yours are the only feelings I care to consider. May I speak plainly, Miss Malloy? This is not flattery, then—only the simplest truth. I've never seen a woman as beautiful as you. If you know men at all, you know I'll fight for the chance to win your regard. You'll let me try?"

His face was clean of guile, his manner open, his words straightforward. He wanted to know her better because of her physical loveliness—the immemorial reason. Candour personified. Treachery was the last thing to be suspected lurking back of that ingenuous front. I'd seen it all before. Some one, playing in this game, was going to be carried off the field broken, perhaps, for life. I held my breath, waiting till Shiela spoke.

She looked square in his eyes. Sir Galahad could probably have met a look like that and returned it. I know that Satan could. Lowth never lowered an eyelash.

"This is not flattery either, Mr. Lowth," she said, "only the simplest truth. I've never seen a thing as masculinely beautiful as you. If you know women at all, you'll know that I'd like to have you try to win my friendship. But not unless you have a soul to match the house it lives in. Your body is magnificent, and straight, and white, I guess; but Pat tells me that a little, hump-backed, carbuncled dwarf dwells in it."

Frankness with frankness, then. He whirled on me.

"About that little Forbush girl, for instance," I shot at him before he could get a word across. And he realized that he hadn't one chance in a million to successfully deny any of the things I had told Shiela of him. So the frank smile died on Denis Lowth's fine mouth, and momentarily another came and took its place, and for the fraction of a second, for the first time in the years I've known him, I saw the misshapen thing that dwelt in his beautiful body peeping out.

"This is a man's world, Miss Malloy," said the misshapen thing, and vanished, leaving beautiful Denis Lowth bowing a bland departure.

"It's a fighting man's world, Mr. Lowth," said

Shiela. "We find our greatest joy in conceding it to that breed. But you've missed the fun of fighting the hardest fight."

So Denis Lowth turned and left us, with a suave and brazen "Au revoir"; but I saw the snarl that twitched beneath his frank, departing smile, and caught the unutterable menace in the last wolfish glance that played, like a spray of poison, over Shiela's supple body. I should have killed him then and there. Instead I stood and stared after his broad straight back as he shouldered his way down the crowded aisle toward the Madison Avenue exits, and was lost. I've heard that humans never become accustomed to a wolf howl; that the hardiest frontiersman, no matter how often he has heard the thing, will feel ice against his spine at the sound of it. I think I felt that same cold chill when Lowth's back disappeared. But, unexplainably, a warm reassurance flowed through me when Shiela and I turned to MacRonan's bench.

Barton had returned. He was standing with his arm about MacRonan's neck, whispering something in the wolfdog's ear, stroking him with a peculiar motion of his hand, upward along the shoulders, so that the great dog's hackle hairs were brushed erect. And as he stroked and whispered, MacRonan's throat rumbled a hell-note and a fiend look out of the black-brown eyes toward the Madison Avenue doorways.

The weather did its very best for us the day we came to visit Barton's kennels. It rained and hailed and sleeted and snowed and blew—Lord help us, how it blew! Old Boreas sat huddled somewhere in the Adirondacks, not fifty miles away, and puffed till his ear drums cracked. Old Boreas with Kabibinoka at his side, wrapped in an icy, sopping Indian blanket. Either of them alone could never have done it. A degree or two of cold would have made the day endurable; but, as it was, the whole world sloshed. Cold rain and soggy snow came howling through stark trees, and over bleak, leprous-spotted fields, and plunged straight down inside the closest of close-drawn coat collars. Slush underfoot, slush overhead, slush in the shrubbery, on the trees. All roofs a-drip with semi-solid clamminess. The very atmosphere a-swash with a devil's stir-about, gone cold and sticky. It took the blowing strength of both of those old windy heathen gods to slap that heavy, blinding plaster in your face.

We had not gone two blocks from the station when the wind-shield of Barton's little coupé was perfectly opaque. Twice we cleaned it, only to find that by the time we reached our seat again, the glass was a blank sheet of thick grey down-sliding mush; so there was nothing to do but to open wide the wind-shield and take it.

At last we came to Barton's country place and the kennels; coated each one of us with seven miles of hurricane-blown slush. We clambered out of the car, half frozen and half drowned. Barton's big, rambling, century-old house said "Welcome" with the loudest voice I ever heard. Bright curtains at the windows.

Smoke struggling upward through the viscid deluge that drove down into the wide chimney-top. I could almost hear the hiss of slush drops on a glowing hickory log. That was the kind of music my mind was tuned to. Lead me to that! But Shiela's mind?

"Where are the kennels?" said that little simpleton. Faith, but that girl's a pig for punishment.

"Weird sister," said I, pinching a bright cheek between a gelid thumb and finger, "I'll have Mr. Barton dig up an old broom for you to straddle if you want to hover through this fog and filthy air—but for me the great indoors. Come on." I dragged at her. But she was anchored fast to Barton's arm; and Barton's feet were planted, ankle deep, in slush. I could see what shape Barton was getting into. Another minute and he wouldn't know but what we were knee-deep in June. They get like that where Shiela is.

"Of course," I said, "if everybody's happy, I'm the last man in northern New York to spoil a party. Let's sit down and be comfortable."

Barton was gone; down for the count. That was as plain as the upper lip on your face. But he laughed just like a normal human being and said, "As far as I'm concerned, this is Miss Malloy's pic-nic."

And so we turned away from that sweetly smoking chimney and made off down a squashy path toward a little grove of trees that flanked the house. And in another moment I was glad we had done it.

A cattle-wire fence some eight feet high enclosed the

kennel run.   At one end of it stood the dog huts, high and well drained, well roofed, dry, comfortable and clean—and not a dog inside of them.   Every last rugged Irish rascal of them was outside, enjoying the pleasant day.

"MacRonan!" called Shiela eagerly.

Did he remember?   Out from behind a clump of lilac bushes he came leaping.   He crashed against the fence, his front paws far above our heads, his great tail waving characteristically, not to and fro, but in a tremendous circle; his eyes a-glitter, his mouth laughing, and a bark like thunder booming at her!   What a welcome!   Puppy?   No, chance.   I could see that.

Barton opened the gate.   "Mac!   Come here!" he shouted.

"MacRonan!" said another voice.

"Look out!   He'll knock you over!" came from Barton as he saw the hound swerve away from him toward the softer call.

I braced the girl against me as the hound leaped for her.   Ferocity was alive in each stupendous bound. A thousand years ago his forbears had been whelped into a service where only the most ferocious were able to survive.   But such affection flamed in those fierce eyes that my heart went warm as the great hound came on.   What a body guard for an Irish princess! Lowth?   A contemptuous breed!   Yseult of Connacht, you would be as safe with him—   Then my foot slipped, and I quit dreaming mighty suddenly as I brought all my strength to bear to keep from going over backward with her under the impact of the dog. Her gloved hands reached high for Skolaun's (MacRonan's, dammit!) neck, and she deliberately buried her rosy face in the great hound's sleet-covered, saggy chest; the wolfdog reared above her; great timbers of his forelegs stretching their shield over her; his head a foot above my own. I'm a tall man. But "in Ireland," says an ancient chronicler, "the animals are smaller than they are elsewhere, except the men, and those hunting dogs called greyhounds."

MacRonan stood behind his cattle-wire fence, looking hard after us, waving his tail in its great circle. I had gotten Shiela away from him and headed at last toward the beckoning smoke finger that that old house was crooking at me. Inside the vestibule a grave and stately lady met us, somehow maintaining a quiet dignity, even though she cavourted a little under the touch of Barton's hand. Not so great a dog as MacRonan by fifty pounds or more. Nowhere near as boisterous and demonstrative. Years and maternity had given her a beautiful reserve. And yet, in her quiet way, she made our welcome to the house just as hearty and genuine as the one with which big Mac had overwhelmed us at the kennels. She sniffed about us very delicately while we removed our sopping outer garments, nuzzled at Barton's hand a bit, submitted with sincere enjoyment to the compliments and caresses that we strangers bestowed on her, and then retired to her place before that hissing hickory log which had been my goal since we alighted from the snow-plastered coupé. I never saw an animal I loved so well on sight. No doubt about it, she was made of finer stuff than Mac. Her colour was somewhere between slate-blue and grey—lovely, but inconspicuous enough to meet the requirements of the deadliest hunter. Mac had the fighter's garb; the tawny red of the lion, marked down the whole length of the spine with a streak of darkest brown—a slash of sombre colour through the solid, rich, red-gold of him, that would bristle in dreadful menace when defence of those he loved called him to battle. But her head, above everything else, was the thing that marked the superiority of this huntress over her warrior mate. It was wonderful; barbed and bewhiskered to a point of savagery that made MacRonan's face appear good-natured. The eyes were deep-set and ringed about completely with a circle of wirelike brows that put into her expression something of the pitiless glare with which the owl, the stealthiest of the predatory birds, fixes his prey. And the deep fire in them!—that could glow with a soft lovelight or scorch with the flaming malignity of a dragon's eyes!

In typical wolfdog fashion she showed me, a little later in the evening, that she was my friend. I called her when we were settled and she came over to me, waving her long tail in evident pleasure. Her head was level with my own as I lay back comfortably in my chair, and she advanced her muzzle slowly, as Mac had done with Shiela, until her nose just barely touched my own. And so she stood a minute, looking deep down into my eyes. Her tail was motionless; her whole body still—although not tensely so. Her tongue stayed in her mouth. Her breath was really held. I never met a gaze so difficult to return steadily and unflinchingly. I think no other dog besides the Scottish deerhound, who is the Irish wolfdog's own blood brother, will look at you so. A great relief came over me as one forefoot raised at last and searched along my chair, though her eyes were still unmoved when I took hold of her huge paw. Then the light of grave inquiry that had reached farther into the soul of me than ever a man had looked went suddenly soft with that great mystery of wistfulness that comes only into the blessed eyes of dogs.

I forced a little laugh.

"Just wait," said Shiela, "till some girl looks fifteen hundred years backward into your eyes, young man. You ain't felt no creeps yet."

All night the storm kept at it. Wind howled. Trees creaked. Wet snow splashed eerily against the panes, as though ghost fingers sought about for the window latches. Lowth was alive somewhere. I couldn't sleep.

I sat up suddenly. Soft steps were on the stair. Upon the landing. In the hall. I lowered my feet noiselessly to the floor and took a step toward Shiela's room. My heart was choking me. Then Barton's voice came to me softly.

"Malloy."

A strangled "Yes" came out of my dry throat.

"It's Aideen. I forgot to tell you. She goes the rounds a few times every night. If your door is open, she'll be in to see you. Perhaps you'd better tell your sister. She might be frightened."

I breathed again.

"I sure was frightened." That was Shiela's voice. She had been awake and heard. "Thanks, Mr. Barton. Pat, will you please unlatch my door for her?"

A minute later I heard the sound of breathing in my room. A low, soft snuffing that would have been inaudible, I think, had I not been listening for it. It came close to my bed and then receded toward the door. There was not the faintest footfall.

"Aideen," I said.

Not till then did I hear a light click of claws on the hard wood. Presently the weight of her head was on the coverlet. I patted her. Next I heard Shiela's voice whispering to her; then the great hound's descent down to her place before the dying fire. Then sleep, secure and untroubled by any dreams of Lowth, fell on me.

Next day the storm still kept it up. Breakfast over, we went out immediately to see the puppies. A lovable quartet of fat and rollicking three-month-olds they were, who tumbled about and squealed and bit and fought good-naturedly among themselves in effort to get under our feet; a bravely staggering, pot-bellied crew, lurching about on enormous, clumsy forepaws, whimpering dog love up to us humans in a way that would have softened the heart of old Bill Sykes himself. But it was easy to see that Shiela's heart was not in that warm, straw-littered kennel house. Her eyes were soft with the feel of those four squirming fur-balls under her hands, but her face was turned toward the back of their stall, where a vapour-clouded window looked opaquely out on to the kennel runs. So out we went into the howling mess. And then it was that I saw that the elements had been kicking up all this row for our especial benefit; for though it was perhaps the most disagreeable day that had ever been foisted upon an innocent and undeserving world, it was a day ideal for one purpose: for first look at Irish wolfhounds in the open.

MacRonan came tearing up the kennel run and through the gate like an Arab stallion; at his side a beautiful seven-months puppy who answered to the lovely name Colleen. The two of them met Aideen on sliding paws, and with a lurch of their great bodies they all three swung away from us, and with big, playful leapings bounded down the path that ran back of the house and made toward an undulating meadow whose white carpet gleamed through a grove of oaks. Moccasins of the Onondagas, like as not, had beaten bare the path that wandered through those ancient boles; but never a craftier hunter nor a mightier warrior trod it than the picturesque savages that ran ahead of us that day. Slate-grey Aideen, a falcon-eyed

Diana; keen brained, wild faced, relentless. Mac-Ronan, war-dog; good nature in his aspect; a warrior who must be roused to do the best within him; but one who, with the battle frenzy on him, would show that inch-long claws and inch-long fangs, when backed by the incredible force of his two hundred pounds, were the tools of absolute annihilation. And Colleen, an adolescent puppy, with the strength and deftness of a full-grown Airedale in her young, galloping body.

Sleet, hail and snow dogs! Storm dogs! A world of tempest and shouting winds the world for them! Wet woods adrip with slush. Misery in the flesh and chill in the bones of men. The animal world standing ashiver, muscles all taut and stiff with the strain of huddling. Not a sign of life. The birds all nested. Not even a corsair of that tough, free-booting sparrow crew a-wing. And out there in that storm-drowned field these three great hounds rejoicing in the weather; racing about with summer-supple muscles. Their harsh coats soaked with icy water; sleet clinging to their brows, ringing their fierce eyes with white. Northern New York was gone for me. Wild, wind-swept moors and sleet-harried bogs of Connacht were before me. Holds of the wolf.

"Here, Mac, Aideen!"

Barton had dropped back, unobserved, until he was some hundred yards behind us; the dogs had gone some hundred yards ahead.

The way those hounds went past! Aideen ahead—a streak of slate against the snow. Greyhound speed

"—*sleet, hail and snow dogs; a world of tempest and shouting winds for them!*"

in her legs. Great Dane strength in her bones. Endless endurance of Scottish deerhound in her deep chest
and her close-tucked loins. Pitiless Borzoi hunting
lust in the snaky slope of her foreface. Greyhound's
hare, Dane's wild boar, deerhound's stag, Borzoi's
wolf: let her keen eye sight any one of these and there
would be blood on the snow—savoury steam thick in
the rafters. Killer—meat-getter! Aideen, you queen
of long-hounds! And one great leap behind her came
MacRonan, the bitch pup at his heels. A little slower
to start—a little longer getting his great bulk under
way—but when he did! Lacking a little the consummate grace of Aideen, he made that up in power. His
iron-armed paws, when his front legs recovered, swung
in an outside circle, loose-centred at the wrist, and
flung forward with a snap to earth that made the cold
mud squirt up from under the snow; and his back legs
filled the air with a streaming fusillade of half-frozen
clods behind him. Something of indolence was in the
easy lurch of his big body—and yet there was not the
slightest lengthening of the space between him and the
flying huntress just ahead. Somehow the feeling would
not down that were he roused—were he hard put to
it—could he be made to lay out flat and straight in
his stride—alter the lurching roll to tense and desperate
effort—he could pass Aideen in twenty jumps. But
as he went careering past Shiela and me my sister
summed up in a question the thing that was most im-
pressive in his running.

"How would you like to try to stop him, Pat?" she

gasped, her hand tight on my arm with the joy inside of her.

Strength, that was it. She had it. Aideen skimmed over the ground. MacRonan took hold of the earth with his strong claws and hurled himself ahead. I would as soon have tried to stop a cheetah. Aideen pursued, remorseless. MacRonan charged, headlong. The foes of old Cormac MacArt must have felt their hearts turning to water in their chests when Finn's battle pack, three hundred of Mac-Ronan's kind, came roaring down on their unarmoured bodies.

"Down, you big rascals!" Barton's voice came muffled through the snow pall, almost lost in the howl of the wind and the clamour of the hounds as they came sliding up to him. Across the field, dim through the storm, we could see the three big brutes reared up above him. The man himself was wholly hidden. We heard his laugh, half good-natured and half rueful, break out as he felt himself going. Then the dim group swayed and suddenly surged to earth as he staggered beneath the weight, slipped and went down.

"We'd be seeing horror, Pat," said Shiela, her quick imagination busy, "were those three hating him instead of loving him."

I thought of a man's chance against either Mac or Aideen alone, and it wasn't the drip of icy water down the inside of my collar that made the skin crawl along my spine.

The hounds were backed away in a riotous triangle

long before we reached him. He rose, a rather ludicrous figure. Great muddy paw marks spotted him all over, and his hands groped ruefully beneath the skirts of his great-coat as he tried to free his skin from the clammy contact of his clothes. Shiela laughed. I tried for an hour or more before I got the common sense to give over the attempt to put that laugh of Shiela Malloy's on a sheet of paper. It's a pity, too, you not to know about it. The second violins rollicking through the scherzo of Mendelssohn's Celtic symphony might give you some idea. I never thought a man could laugh with an icy brooklet running down the broad of his back but there's no escaping some contagions. Even Barton's lugubrious expression faded in a couple of seconds and he too joined Shiela in the rib-shaking music she was making at his expense.

"You're a poor man, Mr. Barton," said my sister, when she could talk, "in bodily comforts; but you've got a third of the riches of the world, so you can well afford to laugh at small annoyances."

"How's that—a third?" asked Barton, still forlornly laughing. "There's more than nine grown wolfdogs in the world."

"Real wealth's not all in wolfdogs. One of Bodb Dearg's old stories has it that a rich man is known by three sounds you hear as you come to his place: 'the noise of men drinking in the house, the grunting of good pigs with the fat thick on their ribs, and the barking of great hounds eager to hunt in the fair green country.' "

"By that standard I'm a rich man this minute," said Barton, "for there's a good pig or two in the pen back of the grove, and what it takes to make men noisy at drink I've got. But I count two other kinds of music necessary to wealth: the sound of the right voice singing in the sunny woman's house and the prattle of children's voices mingled in it." He fixed his two grey eyes on Shiela as he answered her—so steadily that her laughter stopped and she shifted her eyes from Barton to the dogs that barked about him, begging for another romp; whereat he turned to them, too.

"Come on, devils," he said. "Your run is over for today. You've chased me in the house for other clothes, and you don't get me out again till this filthy weather changes."

That evening, just before we retired, he told me what he thought he ought to have to let MacRonan go.

I put it up to Shiela. "Him or the little yellow roadster?" I asked.

Shiela smiled at the utter stupidity of such a question.

"Just one thing, then." I turned to our host. "He isn't ever vicious?"

It was Barton's turn to smile.

"But the way he greeted Lowth," I said.

For answer Barton pointed to a little brown and gold book on the shelves just back of me. I took it out. It was the story of Burnt Najl—that volume of wild old tales of horse-fighting, heathen Iceland, where Gunnar of Lithend and dour young Skarpheddin, two of the finest characters of all literature, hold the pages.

"I think the ribbon is at the right place," said Barton.

I read it. I had known that the Irish wolfhound had gone as a worthy gift from king to king as far as China; but here was a record of him in the old Najl's saga—way up on the edge of the world in that far-off land of ice and fire.

"Then Olaf said to Gunnar, at their parting, I will give thee three things of price, a gold ring, and a cloak that the Erse king owned, and a hound that was given me in Ireland. He is big, and as good a follower as a sturdy man. Besides, it is part of his nature that he has a man's wit; he can see, too, in any man's face whether he means thee well or ill, and he will lay down his life to be true to thee. This hound's name is Saehm."

We all were silent for a while. We all had known that searching wolfdog scrutiny, that creepy eye-to-eye examination. All three of us had heard that terrible warning growl at Lowth.

"Perhaps we can have the roadster too," I said to Shiela, smiling, as I put back the book. Shiela returned the smile. But Barton's face was grave.

"That would be fine," he said. "For Saehm did die for Gunnar—in a hair-raising finish fight. His last breath was a great growl of warning that carried news of treachery to his master."

I slept uneasily that night. Toward daybreak a

great barking out at the kennels roused me. A little later I thought I heard the sound of stealthy footsteps. I listened—and the certainty of it brought me to my elbow. Then I remembered Aideen's watch rounds and fell into a fitful sleep again.

Before breakfast, while I was getting my things together for departure, Barton put his head into my room.

"You've really got to go today?" he asked. I told him "Yes."

"Sleep better?" he inquired.

"No," I answered. "I don't know why. I guess it takes a night or two to get accustomed to Aideen's police rounds."

"Aideen?" said Barton, puzzled. "But I thought of that. Last evening after you two retired I took her out to the kennels for the night!"

Fear shook her Gorgon locks before my eyes and turned me rigid. I knew I should have killed him then and there. Then I shook off the petrifying spell, threw Barton crashing back against the dresser, and plunged through Shiela's door. As I tore back the curtains of that old canopied bed the smell of ether sneaked sickeningly out. I knew I should have killed him. He had seen her—heard her throat's maddening music —touched her; and like a fool I had let him go on living. Why? Fear of the Law? Not that, thank God, nor any other fear. Perhaps under most tests I might prove cowardly enough, but not in any test where Shiela is concerned. Then bravery were simple;

for any fear I might feel for myself would be
totally swept away by fear for her. No fear of anything on the earth's face had kept my hand off of
Lowth. Not even fear of Lowth himself. I had not
killed him simply because such things were not done
in the year of grace nineteen twenty-one. He was
still living,—and the canopy over that empty bed in
which my sister Shiela's clean young body had been
stretched in clean young sleep was giving off the foul
reek of ether, because to have killed Lowth would have
been unusual. Unusual,—God! The stale blood of a
thousand years of civilization crawled feebly through
my veins. But for the pumping of my parents' sturdy
hearts within my heart I think the sluggish stream
would have clotted long ago. Is it a wonder then that
a man will dream sometimes of ancient days; of days
when Maev with her long, pale, lovely face and her
wealth of corn-hued hair, and her tall fire-veined body,
was tigress-queen of Connacht? Had evil hunger, such
as even Lowth's suave smiling had not been able to veil,
gleamed its vile insult in any man's eye at sight of my
slim sister then, I would have thrown a spear through
him without a moment's thought.

And then, in this hour of black depression and sickening despair, Old Ireland, the Ireland of Maev and
Fergus, and Conn the Hundred Fighter, sent help,
real help; no thing of fancy, no dream of old hero
tales to stir a man to deeds; but flesh and blood; flesh
that was tense with lion strength and the lust to try it;
blood that a thousand years of civilization had not

slowed down a whit in its wild, free surging. My own slow blood leaped fresh and hot, and my limp knees snapped straight, as a heavy body leaned against my thigh. And I heard beside me now a sound that had thrilled the hearts of Irish tribesmen back in the dawn of history; the mingling of a whimper of dreadful eagerness with a murder growl; the throat noise of the terrible, nimble wolfdog of the Gael straining against his leash.

I clenched my fingers in the hard hair that bristled on Aideen's shoulders.

"The hounds!" I shouted.

Barton looked at me dumbly. He hadn't realized it yet.

"The housekeeper just brought her in from the kennels," he said blankly.

I calmed my voice to quietness. "Lowth!" I whispered. "He's taken Shiela! I know I should have killed him. But the dogs!"

Then he realized. A stick of chalk drawn across his cheek would not have left a mark.

"But they are sight hounds," he rasped out, his voice cords nearly soundless with the horror.

"He heard me name the date of our visit here when he met us at the show," I said. "But why should he pick your place, Barton?"

And then, at the question, through those two horn-rimmed windows came blazing that metallic light.

"Lowth?" He fairly yelled his eager inquiry.

I nodded.

"Denis Lowth?"

I nodded again.

"Steel king?"

I nodded still a third time, suspense torturing the very soul of me.

His voice had calmed to tones that were quiet and low.

"Want to know why he chose my place?" he asked.

Something ripped loose inside of me some place, and I cursed his slow tongue blasphemously.

He smiled a gentle, tolerant smile; but flint sparks glinted behind his glasses as he spoke.

"He has an Adirondack lodge," he said. "I've seen it. The mountains aren't fifty miles from here."

The three of us leaped for the garage together.

I never saw such driving. We flew along that icy road as though a lunatic were at the wheel. But Barton was as sane as you are now. A madman would have turned us upside-down in the first half mile. Just the same, no normal human being could have driven a car like that. Let's see. Shakespeare groups three abnormal types together. "The lunatic, the lover and the poet"; that's the line. But Barton was no poet, either. Shiela, you black-browed Irish witch! Turn hell-witch, little sister! Turn Morrigu,—Irish battle-fury! Fight! There's three of us on the road; and one who drives with a wilder, surer skill than either lunatic or poet is giving her the gas.

Chains! The whirr of them was in my ears. I

blessed the man who first invented them a dozen times for every mile of that mad ride. I never saw such driving. I've been in cars that had three times the speed of ours; but on that icy road, that day, I would have matched the little thing that carried us against the twelve best cylinders in America. The little devil wasn't good for thirty-five, but when your driver yanks the accelerator down against the stop and leaves it there, you're due to ride. We rode. One dizzy hour we rode. Down grade our speed was only limited by the length and steepness of the hill. Round curves full speed, leaping depressions where the road was bad; scraping past other cars, their driver's curses sounding faint and blurred; into the ditch and out; slithering, jumping, lurching, climbing; we rode. Four sweeter pistons never caught the hammer of flaming gas. Some sixty minutes of soft and perfect motor music. And then those four sweet pistons slowed, found respite from their fiery flogging, stopped. There was no more gas.

Lake Moskwean lay long and narrow, shining smoothly in the ravine, three hundred feet below us. The road had changed from concrete to macadam where we had turned off into the mountains five miles back. It ran along the lake, climbing up steeply, two miles or so beyond us, hair-pinned around the northern end of Moskwean, and then came back along its western side, still climbing sharply, the two legs of the hair-pin not five hundred yards apart.

We started running, but we hadn't gone a hundred

yards from the car when I caught hold of Barton's
arm and dragged him to a stop.

I pointed silently.

From behind a clump of trees that lined the lake
side of the road directly across the water from us, a
long town-car came, labouring at the long, hard grade;
and as we looked, it bucked brutally once or twice,
and stopped.

We dropped behind some brush and held our breath.
A huddled figure in the chauffeur's seat rose up.
Lowth! I would know that marvellous body at five
thousand yards. He scrutinized his engine. We heard
distinctly when the hood came down with a truculent
slam. Then he went out of sight behind the closed
section of the car. A door went 'chunk.' And Lowth
was striding up the mountain road with a limp bundle
draped across his shoulder.

"Aideen!"

The eager eyes glared out along the line of Barton's
pointing finger. Lowth disappeared back of a line of
trees. Sight-hound, we've done our part for you!

"Go kill, you Irish wolfdog!"

Barton's voice, I guess. Quiet and low like Barton's. But hard, hard, hard!

The long road stretched ahead two miles or more,
and made its turn, and came back parallel to itself
across the narrow lake. The lake lay like a silver
serpent sleeping beneath the steep cliffs on either side.

"Watch her,'" said Barton. She was his dog. He
knew her. But she had backed clear across the road

before I saw what Barton wanted me to watch. One great leap carried her across the road. Another took her to the cliff edge.

I gazed down into the deep ravine of Moskwean and saw a thing so beautiful that I have neither the hope nor the desire to match it in this world. The wind had died. The lake was mirror-quiet. Up from the very bottom of the lake; up from the dark, mysterious, unplumbed depths of Moskwean, a giant hound, with dragon eyes and death-fanged mouth, came rushing. It was Bran, the mightiest dog the world has ever known, plunging to Aideen's aid. That was Loch Teernach Bran below me, not Lake Moskwean. Two thousand years ago a snow-white hart with golden hoofs had leaped from a high cliff into Loch Terrnach Bran, with Bran, the fleetest thing in Ireland and the world, close on her flank. And then, once in her element, the yellow-footed hart had changed to a beautiful woman, who laying her hand on Bran's head had drawn him under, never to be seen by sorrowing Finn MacCool again. And now, after those many centuries, at the call of one of her daughters, the mighty Bran had burst the water-witches' enchanted leash and was rushing upward, out of those under-wave caverns, to the help of an Irish girl that had the blood of Irish queens within her.

Shadowy Bran and flesh and blood Aideen met, and the marvellous reflection vanished in a twenty-foot geyser of spray. A moment of anxiety, and then Aideen's wild face came bursting to the surface and her long legs and broad paws started to drive her through the icy lake. Then we turned our faces out toward the hair-pin turn and ran.

She must have swum that quarter mile, and scaled the almost perpendicular cliff in unbelievable time, for it was just as we were rounding the sharp turn at the end of the lake that we heard the shots. One. Two. Three. Four. Five. Then a long, heart-sickening interval. She might be at his throat. He might be cautiously investigating to see if five had done the work. Then,—six! Aideen,—Aideen,—Aideen!

But even six had not quite done it. For when we went gasping past her a few minutes later, she was still crawling forward. One broken fore-leg was under her; one back leg dragging out behind her; her long tail red from trailing limply in the broad blood-path that marked her progress up that snowy slope.

We could not stop. But she would not have had us stop. She raised her head as we came up; but there was no call for help in the black-brown eyes. As yet no death film dulled them. Instead I caught the flashing of that cruel dragon fire, even as weakness brought the proud, wild head down into the snow again. We staggered past the glorious, loyal thing and left her bleeding there, crawling forward to the hunt with the last vestiges of the terrible wolfdog strength that was somehow keeping her alive with enough lead inside her body to stop a lion's heart. Iron of hate put new strength into my sagging knees as we struggled away from her up the steep road that led to Lowth's mountain lodge. He'd pay! I swore by the heathen gods my ancient people swore by that he'd pay!

Barton kept ahead of me although I tried till my tendons cracked to stay beside him. Barton, the student, book worm; Barton, bespectacled, spare shouldered. And yet his daily rompings with his giant hounds had put an unsuspected toughness into him. Then, too, the man with the strongest sinews does not always break the tape. The strongest spirit has the odds. Whatever the cause, I, with the strength of many gridiron seasons still lingering in my legs, saw myself losing ground. And yet I felt no shame; for the girl I was struggling up that icy hill to help was only my sister.

Another minute's straining effort, and I saw Barton turn to the right and vanish in the trees. A dozen aching strides and I had also reached the point from which I could see the beautiful lodge that Lowth had built for himself, up in the woods, a little off the road. I swung in to follow Barton, and then I suddenly wheeled clear about, and held my bursting lungs to quietness a second.

Across the lake the cliffs that sprang from Moskwean's bright mirror soared up above the road as many hundred feet as they dropped downward from the road to the water. The day was still and windless. The cliff a perfect sounding board. A faint sweet sound repeated, and brought my lungs to gasping action again, and set up in my heart a pounding that was not wholly the result of matching Barton's killing pace on those five miles of icy road. There was no mistaking it. The faint clear, clink, clink, clink, came through the trees that hid the road over there where the little coupé stood helpless. My eyes were on the highway where it emerged from behind the fringe of growth, to run for a quarter mile along the bald cliff face.

I knew it. Dog-chain!

Forty odd miles! One hour till the gas gave out. One hour, perhaps, of struggle afoot upon that icy mountain grade. Like a fool, I stood and watched that road across the lake.

There!

He flashed out in the open. The easy indolence was gone out of his stride; the lurching roll flattened to desperate effort. Two hours and more had passed since his steel leash had snapped, and the wire fence had gone down before him. Here was a dog! What his speed must have been for the half hour or so that he was able to keep us in sight, I'd be afraid to guess. But I know that any heart less tough than an Irish wolfdog's would have burst with the effort he must have made to keep us in his vision. But chain tracks on a newly travelled snowy road are easy to follow, and so I could picture this great sight-hound finally stretching his body between these parallel dark lines that his wise brain associated with the thing he was pursuing, and setting himself a pace that would let him follow them as far as they might go.

Some intuition must have told him to go on by the empty car, for now his lion-coloured body was leaping along the silver background of the icicled cliff, toward the turn in the road. Music flowed out of that mighty running; such stately grace was in it, such indescribable beauty, such irresistible and majestic rhythm, such dreadful strength. Grace and beauty and rhythm and strength such as Chopin wrote into his terrible war-polonaise. As I watched MacRonan charging to our aid, the chords of that thundering music surging through me, the whole road back of him seemed suddenly to fill with leaping forms. The fearful battle-pack of King Cormac MacArt seemed to be springing along that icy cliff. Three hundred sets of lion jaws a-slaver; three hundred pairs of dark eyes flashing dragon-fire; three hundred deep throats snarling their frightful challenge! Bran and Skolaun, Conbec and Adnuall, Seang the slim, Aluinn the handsome, Torann the thunderer; these and their brotherhood of mighty hounds whose beautiful names and hero deeds sparkle on every page of Irish legend. A mighty company not to be seen in Adirondack hills nor in the whole world anywhere in this year of grace nineteen twenty-one.

MacRonan plunged out of my sight into the trees, and the ghost-pack that had filled the quarter mile of open road behind him vanished. Dreams, young Malloy! Dreams, you fool! And a good half minute of time more precious than any you've ever lived, gone,—wasted! And yet I think my body flung itself up the stone path to Shiela's help with a fresh strength that maybe even Barton could not have matched.

He was bruising his shoulders against the stout oak door when I got to him. Just once I tried it with him. There was no more yield to it than to the thick stone walls in which it made a portal.

The shutters were all closed and barred and locked; except at one end of the house. There high up on each side of a broad based chimney, two small decorative windows, made of lead and rich stained glass, not openable, were unprotected. The rough stones of the chimney made ideal footing. A couple kicks; a huddled leap; and I was sprawling on a leopard rug amid the litter of the table I had landed on. Lowth stood by a couch on which my sister lay, and flipped into place the cylinder of a long black service pistol as I rose.

"If you had only waited until I finished this reloading," he said, "I would have opened the door for you."

I heard the thump of Barton dropping to the floor behind me.

"I never saw such wonderful vitality," said Lowth. 'I had to use every chamber of the gun,—and I shoot very well."

Barton took one step past me.

"Malloy will find out just how well I shoot if you move again," said Lowth, quietly, without a trace of malice in his voice.

Barton went stiff.

"The situation is a very simple one," Lowth went on. "If one of you advance, I kill the other. Uninvolved, isn't it? Even Malloy should comprehend it."

I reached out a stealthy hand and tried to push Barton ahead; but he must have been expecting that, for he was braced. He turned to me and shook his head.

"I can't," he said. "He has us."

I racked my brain for a reason why he didn't shoot us both without a second's delay; and could only think of one. Perhaps he really hadn't found the time or the ammunition to reload that gun.

"That damned revolver isn't loaded, Barton,—go and get him!"

"If you're so sure of that," said Barton, "why don't you go and get him?"

And I stood rooted.

"You see?" said Barton.

And yet one thing I couldn't see: why he should hold his fire. I knew the man. He had there on the couch beside him the thing he had been wanting all his black life: a woman he couldn't win. Women had yielded to his wealth, to the strength and beauty of him, to his honeyed tongue, to his brilliant brain. But here was one that the combination of his powers over women could not move. Only one thing would make her his; the pure brute strength of him. She lay where he had flung her; breathing heavily; her senseless figure twisted into helpless, beautiful lines that few bodies would have had the suppleness to assume. The pale warm colour of her shone through her thin nigh dress. A rope of blue-black hair hung down across her throat and trailed out on the floor. One white foot hung limply,—profiling against the dark upholstery of the couch curves at instep and at arch such as kingdoms have been wrecked for.

Tomorrow she would be a tiger-cat. Strong in body; wild in spirit. Magnificent in hate and desperation. She would fight with brain and muscle, teeth and nails. He had sought for a woman like that all his black life.

And here were two inferior, insignificant things that stood between Denis Lowth and what he wanted only because they were living things. A couple finger twitches; two weighted sacks; a straight cliff dropping sheer into a lonely, bottomless mountain lake! I could see only one reason why my heart and Barton's were still pounding.

"We might as well be comfortable, don't you think?" said Lowth politely.

He picked up a match-box holder from the floor and stepped toward the fireplace. Great logs and kindling were in place. Lowth flung a burning match into the carpet of pine needles that covered the hearth.

It was all a play for time. A minute or two in which to solve this difficulty of the empty gun. He could have killed us both bare-handed; but the thing must be more quickly done than that, for Shiela's breathing was taking on a quick, spasmodic quality that showed she would be conscious presently; and he would not have the fighting spirit of her broken by sight of the horror of a death fight between men armed with the dreadful arms of the weaponless.

It was all a play for time. I knew it. Yet, if I leaped, that gun would swing on Barton,—and maybe— So we stood, poor devils that we were; not as much brains in our two heads as in his one,—outwitted.

Then came a quiet, cruel smile over Lowth's face. He had us. He had decided. How he was going to do it, I will never know. But he had us,—sure. There was absolute certainty in that smile. Barton saw it too.

"Good luck, Malloy!"

I heard the whisper under his breath and knew that he was going to leap:—the grey-eyed, rim-spectacled, master of wolfhounds! And I knew at the same time that it took a greater bravery to leap than to stand still and wait.

I drew a breath, and braced myself, so that if there really was a bullet in that gun, it would not knock me down; so that, if his aim failed of a vital hit, I should be on my feet and ready to make a try. And as I waited, ears keen for the scuffle of Barton's feet, it came,—the thing I waited.

Lowth's face went pale as death. Lowth was afraid! I felt an insane banshee laugh rising inside of me. His eyes were the eyes of a hunted thing. Lowth,— Denis Lowth,—was afraid,—afraid! Afraid of that sound of scratching at the door!

The gun dropped clattering on the hearth.

I knew it! I knew it hadn't been reloaded.

"I hit her every time!" came gurgling out of Lowth's constricted throat. He thought it was Aideen!

Just then glass tinkled to the floor. Lowth whirled about; his back to us. He never was afraid of us anyway. He faced the shattered window; and as he did, fright put a withered arm about his neck, dipped a ghost-cold hand down deep into his chest, and laid a caress like that of some dead and decaying strumpet's rigid fingers on his heart.

I swear I couldn't look. I turned from the ghastly sight and followed his glance instead. The window sill was more than six feet from the floor; but above it, something was looking in! A berserk. No dog's eyes ever brimmed with fire as fresh from hell as that! A werwolf's might.

A head came through, framed in the jagged splinters of crimson glass. The flaming eyes found Lowth. And a dreadful hunger, dormant a thousand years, filled up the mouth with venom—venom that frothed through anlace teeth and over a lolling tongue, to splash on the floor with a viscid drip,—drip,—drip,—drip,— drip,—drip. Six drops; loud as six pistol shots in the perfect quiet,—then that dragon face withdrew, was gone. Call him MacRonan if you want. I know Skolaun of Ballycoordin when I see him.

We waited. I watched the crimson window, breathless. So did Lowth.

"He won't try that." I'll never hear anything quite so matter-of-fact if I live a thousand years. "He saw me," Barton said. "Their strength is unbelievable, but they never waste it;—except in play. He has come far. He'll take the easiest way to get inside."

He was right. Lowth whirled again before he had finished speaking. He well might whirl—and crouch—and gather together the shattered fragments of his strength; for there, again, was that scratching at the door.

Barton turned and took a step, but I caught him by the shoulder. I knew his arms were aching with hunger for her.

"You get her out of the way," I said.

He stooped to pick her up. Even with my little sister lying twisted in her night dress there, the year of grace nineteen hundred and twenty-one would not let go its hold on me.

"I thank Saint Patrick's God I'm not the one that has to kill you, Lowth," I said, and meant it.

But way down deep inside my heart some fine old gloating heathen god kept up his banshee laughter, and while Lowth crouched afraid—afraid, curse his black soul—I walked across the room, slipped back the latch, and flung the door wide open.

Fur Chaser

Rabbits!

That was the trouble with El Paso Don. Not that such frailties are unforgivable. Each of us has his weakness. Ming porcelains. Old masters. Toy dogs. Golf. Strong men play volley ball while gallows' ropes rot. So long as our foibles keep to the hobby level, all is Jake. But Don got his standard of values all messed up;—made fur his vocation, feathers his avocation.

Don was a pointer dog. A pointer dog to your good old heart's content! Bone and muscle and brain, speed and endurance and clean-cut beauty were Don's; and an Irish wolfdog's heart; and a noise. Holy sweet-smoking Tophet, what a nose!

Birds were Don's business. Chicken or quail, pheasant or grouse, woodcock or snipe; let any one of them come within seventeen miles of Don's sweet sniffer, and that bird was a goner, plucked and cooked, served and the bones picked bare. No chance a-tall. Head up, tail swinging, gait free and easy, you'd see Don's long, ground-eating gallop drop to a trot as his nose came round to the wind; the trot slow down to a walk. Then up through the frosty grass he'd march like a grenadier. Whango! Don had 'em!

"Come out of it, Don, you doggone fool!" low voiced. "We haven't seen a bird today. This blasted country's as featherless as a toad. Ain't you got fun now, standing there like a mullet-head, pointing land turtles. Go on! There's no quail in that ragweed."

A sly, half-humorous glance up at you out of those bright brown eyes, brows lifted ever so little in the act. Aside from that a dog of liver-spotted marble, nose to stern.

"How come, go on? Say, listen, boss,—you shoot these birds. I'll find 'em. Sure there's quail!"

Try moving him. Pick him up even, clear off his feet. Turn him a hundred and eighty degrees. Just as you put him down, so he stays put; an image. Only the clean neck bends, letting the head turn stealthily till that flaming ragweed clump is in the line of fire of his deadly nose again. Might as well move up, unlimber your guns, and kick 'em out. If Don says birds, then birds! With one exception,—

Rabbits!

Doc Holden was a firm believer in the theory that a bird-dog puppy should be allowed to learn the ways and wiles of feathered game by his own methods. Self-hunting, bird men call it. Turn the pup loose. Let him run his ears off. Time enough in a year to restrict his natural methods with commands after untrammelled days of self-hunting have built up the ranging spirit and the natural bird wisdom of him.

So, acting on his beliefs, Doc picked out the likeliest son of Doctor's Girl and sent him to Eddie Garfield, down in Alabama, with instructions to Friend Ed to throw away the leash. Ed gave the pup a week to get acquainted with his big quail-stocked preserve and then cut the rope; and the pup, standing not upon the order of his going, went away from there at once— and stayed; vanished as though the soil of the Cotton State had gobbled him down, hide, heels and tail. Buggy wheels whirled all over Northern Alabama. Wires grew hot from Maine to Florida. Detectives searched. Dog papers printed fabulous offers of reward. A puppy out of Doctor's Girl by Apache Don was lost or strayed or stolen. Pointer men's hearts skipped a beat or two for half a year thereafter at the sight of every stray, battered, liver-spotted dog that padded by. Then by degrees the commotion died.

And so at last, in solemn conclave, tearful by fifty per cent and maybe more, Doc Holden and his insufferably good-looking daughter Madge decided that there was to be no further heartache over Don. This decision made, with as much firmness as though there were some sense in it, Doc and his daughter arose from the davenport in Doc's book-walled den and proceeded to the kennels, there to go bravely about the business of picking out El Paso Don's successor as a field-trial winner. And on this day, as they stood there with elbows on the kennel fence, doubtfully appraising those of Don's litter brothers and sisters who still dwelt at the Holden huts, at the self-same hour, like as not, Ed Garfield, after long and hopeless searchings, found much as Sir Launfal did, the thing he sought for, right at his castle gate.

Ed was returning from a weary, rumour-goaded quest out in the sticks—his horses mired to the ears, his buggy wheels mud-disked, his spirit resting like nine pounds of bird shot at the bottom of his high-laced field boots, and no more liver-spotted dog beside him than a pollywog. As he coaxed his tired sorrels up the lane that leads to his wide-rambling, long-columned house he heard, back in the scrub pine, off to his left, a mellow tonguing. Pooh for that! Beagles! Without a pause or look he kept clucking to his horses; but a little further on he came upon an ancient and decrepit darky, with an ancient and decrepit howitzer laid across his knees, hunched in a seemingly dejected knot on the top rail of a snake fence, watching with rheumy and lacklustre eyes the small pine grove whence the tonguing came, clearer and closer every second. Ed pulled up.

"What luck today, uncle?" asked Eddie sociably, something in the old fellow's stuck-in-the-slough expression striking a kindred note in the white man's gloomy heart. And in answer uncle leaned rheumatically forward and hauled up out of the grass half the rabbits in Jackson County.

"Great shades of Nimrod!" shouted Ed. "How can

an old nigger like you tramp enough ground to gather in a bag of cottontails like that?"

The old man shifted a bit.

"Ain' tramp no groun', cap'n," he grunted amiably. "Ol' Eph jus' set heah on de fence an' roll 'em. Oscuh, he race 'em roun'. Oscuh's de rabbit-huntin'es' dawg in Alabam'. W'en all de hoppers in dishyer county's done brung roun', Oscuh's gon' trabl' oveh in de nex' an' race dem all up in front ol' Come-to-Pappy too."

He patted Come-to-Pappy on the battered stock.

"Hol' fas' de reins an' watch a li'l, cap'n," he continued, grinning. "Gon' crack down on ol' mule-ears in a secon'."

The tonguing in the grove of pines grew deeper and more musical, and Uncle Eph yanked back two murderous-looking hammers; and presently to the accompaniment of the sweetest beagle music Ed had ever heard a ball of fur bounced out of the cover, hopping desperately up to Come-to-Pappy's muzzles; and, indistinct in the high grass, the biggest rabbit hound that Ed had ever seen was yelling his head off not a sixteenth of an inch behind that bunny's cotton end.

Uncle pulled up his harquebus and sighted with watery eyes along its rusty barrels. From where Ed sat it looked as though the rout of pickaninnies at Eph's cabin had a fine chance for dog giblet along with their rabbit stew that night.

And then, just as the darky pressed the trigger, Ed

leaned far out from his buggy seat and made a wild grab at him.

"Don't shoot, for the love of Stonewall Jackson!" bellowed Ed.

"Dow!" roared the ancient culverin. And workmanlike as any job the jolly old black-hooded craftsman ever put over at the block with his two-handed snickersnee, Eph sliced that cottontail's head plumb off at the shoulders.

Ed checked his dancing horses, rubbed his eyes and swallowed hard.

"Uncle," he asked, gulping at the holy fright that choked up his throat, "don't you take an awful chance, killing that close in front of your hound?"

"Done gotta," the old man explained. "Done gotta roll dem hoppers right out f'om undeh dat Oscuh's nose. Dat's how he bring 'em by. Ol' man ain' take no chance though," he added, grinning lofty pride of craft. "Ain' no chance business with ol' man an' Come-to-Pappy. Dead shuah we knock dem jackass ears loose ev'y time."

Eddie Garfield meantime had come to a decision. Thinking of the astonishing figures that the dog magazines had printed half a year before, Ed reached for his wad. Ed loved old darkies as Southerners know how to love them.

Most of us folks up here in the snow belt would have given the old man a twenty-dollar bill and called it square, quite satisfied with his elation and our own sense of munificence and honesty.

"Oscar's his name, is it?" inquired Ed.

"Yessuh."

"Find him?"

"Yessuh. Come in one day las' summeh with my otheh dawgs. Stayed along."

"Been hunting rabbits with him ever since?"

"Eveh since de season open," Eph answered circumspectly.

"Great codfish balls!" groaned Ed.

"Yessuh," replied Eph with rare intelligence. "How come?"

"For sale?"

"Nossuh, cap'n," Eph made emphatic answer. "Dem pickaninnes's gotta eat."

Ed always carried sinews of war aplenty on his various excursions on the trail of Doc Holden's pointer pup. So he was able now to produce, for uncle's benefit, a roll of bills big enough to plug a city sewer. He started to peel that wad very slowly, one luscious green skin at a time. Eph cleared a constricted throat.

"Always could get my share of rabbits with dem ol' houn's befoh dis Oscuh dawg eveh come," he muttered, weakening.

Ed kept on peeling. Ed was thinking. At last he had it. Those of us up here where the ice grows who would have had the honesty to turn over that reward to the old fellow would have made the blunder of giving it to him all at once.

"Listen!" said Ed. "I'm Captain Garfield. That's

my house over yonder. How would you like to come to my place every Saturday morning and get a large round iron dollar?"

The ancient gentleman of colour looked his incredulity. Yet this man, it seemed, was Cap'n Ed Garfiel'. Cap'n Ed, so he had heard many and many a time, never lied to a nigger.

"Ev'y Sat'day mo'nin' I comes to you-all's place an' gets a dollah?"

"That's it."

"Wha' fo'?"

"For that dog."

"No wuhk?"

"No work!"

"Fo' how long I gets dishyer dollah ev'y Sat'day mo'nin'?"

"Forever. This is Friday. Here's a dollar to start us off right. But come around tomorrow for another."

Shaking his cotton-thatched head at the incomprehensible ways of white folks, Eph took from about his shoulders the frayed rope that had answered for Oscar's leash these many months, and with a sigh of mingled delight and resignation handed it to Ed.

"Cap'n," asked Eph as Ed started to stuff the fat roll back into the pocket whence it had come—"Cap'n," asked Ephraim Terwilliger Joppey, licking his lips at thought of certain squat bottles lately offered for sale at his shanty by a weazel-faced white gentleman, "instead of dis heah dollah-a-week business, couldn't you make it six dollahs an' fifty cents in cash?"

And so it came about that while Eph Joppey shuffled down a muddy lane in Jackson County with eight hundred and sixteen rabbits slung under his arm, but minus his dog and with cash assets lacking just five dollars and fifty cents of the purchase price of a bottle of poisonous squareface; and while Doc Holden and his appallingly decorative daughter Madge leaned sorrowfully over a kennel fence way up in New York State, a jubilant gentleman answering to the name of Edward Corson Garfield knelt in gumbo and cursed gleeful words of welcome home into the thin leather of a big-boned, loose-shouldered, lion-hearted, liver-and-white pup that was the rabbit-huntingest dog in Alabama.

Meet Shirleigh Welles. But wait a minute. Bow and say something pretty; but don't shake hands. Don't do it. There's a reason. Shirleigh Welles, if you can grasp the meaning, was one sockdolager of a Waldo, a he tea hound. Shirleigh had shoulders eleven feet across, and the dearest sideburns. Shirleigh had a hoisting-engine boiler for a chest, and polished finger nails. The bottom buttons of Shirleigh's silken vest sunk deep into the splendid cave-in at his waistline. His hips were narrow and immaculately tailored. And the bulging thews of his thick thighs threatened to come cracking through his grey-striped morning trouserettes at every step. But the walk! Sweet marjoram, did you get the walk? "Fifth Avenue!" said the right foot every time it swung forward; and "Watch me, ladies!" said the left. Elbows akimbo just a trifle; arms stiffened; body bent forward at the belt; wide shoulders taking turns at thrusting aggressively ahead,—right leg, right shoulder; left leg, left shoulder; you know that stuff. Gaze inflexible along the line of that truly miraculous progress. Head poked forward and pulled in, in perfect synchronism with each shoulder thrust, much like the pompous progress of Lord Chanticleer, than whom there is no more damfooler insect. And the knee action! Help! Rooster there, too. How do they manage to get like that? Flat-topped iron skimmer resting on ears and eyebrows. Spats. Stick. Fawn suède gloves! Monocle? (No, no! For shame! This is a yarn about dogs and human beings.) Go-to-hell coat? Right you are, Roger! Now you've got him. You hold him till I go get a stone. But get a good hold, buddy; because there's two hundred and eight pounds of him, stripped!

Shirleigh came rooster-strutting down the line of irregular flat stones set in the lawn that led from the Holden house to the kennels just as Doc Holden and his outrageously ornate daughter were commiserating each other on the fact that no field-trial champion's qualities were visible to the naked eye among the pointer pups that now nosed, whimpering along the wire fence. By way of mutual consolation Doc had slipped an arm about his daughter's waist. Any man who has ever seen Madge Holden can name offhand eight thousand more unpleasant activities for the human arm. So, too, no doubt, could Shirleigh Welles. At any rate his speech supports this supposition.

"I just popped in to propose to Madge again," Shirleigh announced, "and Williamson shooed me through back here."

He extended a hand to Doc, smiling meanwhile a smile which was intended to convey good-natured banter, but which, due to the sort of features out of which it was manufactured and to the kind of mind behind the features, only succeeded in carrying to the doctor an impression of about two hundred and eight pounds of ego.

Doc looked at Shirleigh, and smiling as one who bides his time unwound his arm from its delectable resting place and put both hands behind his back.

"Give it to Madge," he said. "She's saving them. I tried it once."

So Shirleigh swung his mighty manicured flipper toward the lady, who without hesitation placed her soft fingers in it.

Back of Doc Holden's good-natured refusal of Mr. Welles' proffered hand there was a reason; based not so much upon the difference between the forearms of the two men as upon the difference between the men themselves. Doc had an arm that could, perhaps, put as much smash into his hand-grasp as could that of Mr. Welles, and that's saying something; for Shirleigh

Welles, without doubt, dangled one nasty whip off his right shoulder. A whip well fitted for such business as that in which Doc Holden's thick and vigourous fifty-year-old wing had just now been engaged. Well-practiced, too it was, in that particular business, we may as well own up; as is often the case with such arms as have had experience in the carnal delights of cutting 'em down after the interference has been flattened out. But Doc Holden was entirely willing that one girl, Nance Holden, Madge's mother, still very much a girl with the forty mark left behind, should, out of a long and happy experience, be the sole testifier as to the efficiency of his good right as an aid to courtship; which was the difference between the men. Mr. Welles for his part didn't care how many ladies, out of shorter and less permanently happy courtships, could testify as to the sterling worth of his good right. Many of these ladies, in point of fact, had no desire to say anything for publication one way or another; but this made little difference to Shirleigh. Shirleigh was noted for his ability to do his own testifying on every occasion when the opportunity arose.

Not in language, mind you. Far be it from Shirleigh. Not in braggart speech. My word, Old Egg, nothing so crass as that! By other means. And because he did not peddle his wares in words, poor Shirleigh laboured under the delusion that his mountainous conceit was unobservable. For instance, to get back to good right arms, Shirleigh had a braggart hand-shake. Doc Holden, as he said, had tried it once. Sufficiency. "Pleasetomeetcha," you would probably say on meeting Shirleigh, and unless warned innocently put forth a hand and exchange grips with a rock crusher. Just as you were about to close your fingers in an honest, white man's hand-clasp, Shirleigh would fling the whole force of that tremendous, inter-ference-smearing shoulder down through arm, fore-arm and wrist, and like some silly gorilla, maim you where you stood; and stand there imbecile and insult-ing and watch you writhe. If he had used that mighty hand-shake as a joke, all could have been for-given. But humour?—in Mr. Welles' make-up? Ha, ha! The thing was braggadocio, pure and simple.

"Shirleigh Welles," that idiot grip would say, with ponderous and bone-bending emphasis. "Welles, you know. Oughty-ought. The champion Scarlet team. All-American four years. You've heard of me. Some arms I've got, eh, what? You poor hundred-and-seventy-five-pound shrimp!"

Superiority was all that asinine performance meant to Shirleigh. Heartiness? With Mr. Welles? Doc Holden had walked quietly away from Shirleigh after his first and only contact with that grip, and with the tears of pain still on his cheeks had headed for an athletic outfitter's. There he bought a spring-grip dumb-bell. Two years later his right forearm was an inch and a quarter bigger round than his left; but he still smiled the smile of one who bides his time whenever Mr. Welles, on his frequent calls at the Holden establishment, offered him, as it were, the good right hydraulic forging press of fellowship.

"What cheer?" asked Shirleigh blithely as he reluctantly allowed Madge Holden to withdraw her hand. "Any bright word from the lost, strayed or stolen?"

Shirleigh, it seemed, would never learn that the loss of a potential field-trial winner is not a matter for blitheness. Doc Holden took his usual second look at this magnificent dandy. Nup! He wouldn't do. Too bad. Doc would have liked to see his daughter marry that million dollars. Why not? A laudable ambition for any man to see his daughter marry a million dollars; provided of course,—and there was the rub. What the devil good is a million dollars to a man if he doesn't love pointer dogs? And, besides, at the trials last year Madge had met a young handler by the name of Thorplay, who had come to a certain meet with five pointer puppies all of the same litter, and, unprecedented in dog history, had carried four of them through to the second series' running of the derby. A man has got to have his heart in pointer dogs to put across a trick like that. Dad could see that million slipping. Dad, in fact, was helping to put the skids beneath it. Love me, love pointer dogs. Madge Holden's happiness was worth ninety-four of the finest million dollar bills you ever laid your eyes on.

"No news," Doc answered Shirleigh. Doc did not know that at that moment a young man down in Alabama was pulling his knees loose from the gumbo and hot-footing it for the nearest telegraph station. "And in this case we call that bad news," and he turned and looked down over the kennel fence again.

The better part of a year had laid its formative fingers on the lithe bodies of the litter brothers and sisters of El Paso Don that now raced, barking, up and down the kennel run in puppy effort to express their appreciation of a visit from the house. But Doctor's Girl, mother of thoroughbreds—and what prouder title is there for the gentler half of any species?—stood quietly now, with her front paws high on the kennel-yard fence, and poked her big squared-off muzzle under the soft hands of her mistress. In eight full years of maternity this fine pointer lady had given to sportsmen ten thousand actual dollars' worth of bird dogs; and approximately ten million dollars' worth of clean American fresh air to hosts of canvas-coated men who at one time or another had tramped behind her splendid progeny over stubble field and prairie on innumerable fine October mornings.

"It seems a shame," murmured the girl, returning with moist hazel eyes the look of steadfast love that shone up to her from grave dark ones. "She's come so close, so often, to mothering a field-trial winner. And yet another litter would almost certainly shorten her life. And I wouldn't give a year of Girl's life for all the field champions in America."

Doc Holden looked down at the precious chestnut head against his shoulder.

"I would!" Doc stated unexpectedly.

The lady tilted up, in question, what is perhaps the most disconcerting chin in the annals of her sex.

"The value of a litter of thoroughbred pointer pups," said her dad in answer to questioning eyes that were still more disturbing than the chin, "is almost invaluable to the good old U. S. A. Game savers, every one. Conservers of the birds that entice men off of office chairs, out of jammed towns, into the haunts where the dollar mark attains its lowest visibility. Such things as that mean more to us than even a year of Girl's devotion, don't they, Young Fellow?"

Doc Holden, veterinary, dog man, true sport, outdoorser, knew a thing or two. He knew for instance that the keenest-nosed dogs afield will sometimes run right over a closely huddled, freshly lighted quail; and knew that the theory was erroneous which held that a lately flushed, scared bird could voluntarily withhold its scent. A swift flight on beating pinions through the crisp air of fall,—and the scent was gone, washed out for a little while; that was all. Doc knew it. So with men, Doc contended. A day of freshness; close to strong broad fields and gallant little birds, and the pungent, aromatic scent of the great American smacker, an odour somewhat sickening when too strong, is gone; washed out for a little while at least,— to the everlasting benefit of mankind.

The Young Fellow, without answering her father's question, watched him with that look of adoration in her face which a girl carries for the father who can look his daughter's mother square in the eye.

"This thing decides us, Madge: will the next litter improve the breed? With her vitality having topped the rise, with the mating fire glowing lower in her, would her next puppies burst with pointer life, blaze pointer courage, glow the deep quiet flame of stubborn pointer endurance, flash pointer brains, dazzle with pointer loveliness? You and I are good pointer men, Madge Holden. That's what decides us."

Doc reached a hand down to the sleek head under his daughter's fingers.

"No more maternity, eh, Girl?" he asked. "Birds and the fields for you from this day forth. Have I got the right dope, you old huzzy? No more worries or responsibilities. And after a while a chair before the fire, waiting; without tremour in that pointer heart of yours, though you'll know perfectly the thing that's coming. We'll put it up to you, old lady. Which is it for the next years, birds or pups?"

At the first mention of the word "birds" the needle-tapered stern had started to fling wildly back and forth; and at its repetition the whimpering in the old dog's throat changed to a choking rumble that culminated suddenly in a series of deep-mouthed, explosive pointer barks.

"The Ayes appear to have it. Birds!" said Doc. The barking turned hysterical. "The Ayes have it! So ordered!" And announcing this decision, Doc returned his arm to such an occupation as would have converted the oldest, sourest, dried-up-est misogynist that ever misoged.

If he had tried for fifty years Shirleigh could not have picked a better time than this particular pointer-surcharged moment to pull the thing that proved he had a very bad Charley horse above his ears.

"My golly-whiz," cursed Shirleigh horribly, "why the salt tears, Madge? Why not get to work on one of the pups you've got and forget that Don dog? They're all the same breeding, aren't they?"

Doc Holden stared, then smiled. His daughter stared without smiling. Forget the Don dog?

"Of course you don't know pointers, Shirleigh," Doc explained. "But one look into that kennel run tells you that there isn't a trial dog in the lot. Nice gun dogs, splendid hunters, plenty of bottom to them all. But there does not flame in a single pair of those brown eyes the unbreakable courage that makes a champion in the field."

"Courage?" said Shirleigh, lifting his eyebrows in his superior stare. "Courage?" he questioned, and for good and all dumped over his apple cart as far as his chances with Madge Holden were concerned. "I'm a great lover of courage myself," Shirleigh explained. "Polo, football, the ring, and what not, have claimed my attention for years. I've even owned a pit dog or two. Paid well to have them trained and handled in the pit. Won ever so many wagers on them until they were killed. Wonderful courage there

—wonderful. Fight till their last drop of blood is
drained."

Shirleigh must have seen Madge Holden shudder.
But Shirleigh was parading the red corpuscles of his
blood before the ladies, and he went on—to his doom.

"But all this talk of dog courage that I hear about
the Holden place—I don't get it. What is there to
build courage in a fifty-pound dog who all his life and
for long generations of forefathers has hunted timid
little two-pound birds?"

Madge Holden looked a scorn that would have
withered any gentleman less self-centred than Mr.
Welles. Madge Holden's soft lips parted for speech.
Madge Holden's lips are no thing to be passed by
without comment; much in effect like this stuff novo-
caine that the dentists shoot you with; block off, as
the medicos put it, whole sets of nerves, leaving a
man temporarily without the necessary stimuli for
speech or motion, while his nerves of sight function
with abnormal intensity.

"Most men, Friend Shirleigh," stated those lips,
"have got to work. Mighty few of our fellow citizens
have the wherewithal for a string of ponies or a college
education and its numerous advantages, including football. Pointers and setters also have a job of work.
They hunt birds for a living. Don't think for a minute, Shirleigh, that because a man's daily job doesn't
demand a halfback's spectacular courage he can't produce the goods when called on. Same with bird dogs.
Answer me this thing, Shirleigh: Who changed

Heinie's goosestep to a quickstep as he scuttled for his hole ten miles behind the Rhine—the champion pug who stayed at home or the necktie salesman who went across?"

The hazel eyes shot fire with the question and the soft lips shut in a tight, straight line. Shirleigh Welles' million-dollar map grew blanker, marvellous to say, than usual. Doc Holden's outdoor tan went red with a suppressed desire to bellow "Attaboy, Madge!" And then as though the old dog-loving vet's cup of gloats were not already full to spilling, a scrawny, gray-uniformed boy climbed his front-porch steps and pushed a button.

Williamson came waddling out to the kennels with a yellow envelope on a tray.

"How much?" asked Doc, reaching for the communication with one hand and into a trousers pocket with the other.

Williamson broke the news.

"How much?"

Williamson repeated the shock. Doc drew back his hand and blew against the finger tips.

"Burnie-burnie!" he exclaimed, and stuck the scorched digits into the other pocket. "Tell the boy to take this wire up to John D.'s place. He can afford to read it."

"Begging your pardon, sir," Williamson ventured, "but I paid the lad out of my own pocket. I was quite anxious, sir. You see the wire is from Alabama. Young Don, sir—the pup, sir—I thought perhaps—"

But the envelope was open. Doc read. Doc gave a leap. Doc's hand came up out of his pocket, clutching a fat, moth-eaten, brass-mouthed wallet, which he shot at Williamson.

"Don't stand there like some big, tame, red-necked baboon, Willy," Holden roared, "but catch that angel boy and give him the biggest bill you can find in that old nickel gripper. Advise him to spend it all on chewing tobacco and cigarettes and Diamond Dicks. Tell him I love him, and embrace him for me. Come on, Delicate! Step out! Pop into it!"

Delicate made for the house as fast as a sixty-inch waist and a butler's dignity would permit. But at the door he turned.

"Don, sir?" he called back in a tone of positive anguish.

"Don, sir," his employer answered in slow and lugubrious accents whose every drawl and pause must have tortured the pointer-loyal soul of 'Enery Williamson. Don, sir, according to this little telegram from some party unknown who signs himself 'Ed,' of Jackson County, state of Alabama, seems to be sitting on top of the world giving battle to a ten-yard string of wienerwursts. Now you get the hell out of here and catch that boy or I'll hop over there and give you a big fat kiss."

Williamson disappeared; but as he romped like some festive hippopotamus through the long wide hall toward the front of the house, the light of his smile gilded the walnut ceiling beams.

"Listen to this."

Doc Holden set his specs on his nose and took a deep breath.

Got Don. Hot damn, you old Doc Holden, and repeat. Eph Joppey's twenty-one black children and grandchildren have been living on bunny pie for six months. Eph has the seven best rabbit runners in the South. Four hound dogs, two half-breed beagles and El Paso Don; named in reverse order of excellence. Some cotton chaser, Don; but, nursie dear, the shape he's in! Wide? The judges will have to follow that baby in an aëroplane. Six weeks till the Southwest trials. No time to lose. Sending him down to Dan at once. Leave it to Dan to knock that fur idea out of his head. Long telegram, but who gives any damns? We live but once and besides, I'm sending this collect and proud to do it Whoops, my beloved!   Ed.

Doc turned to Shirleigh Welles.

"Shirleigh," said he, "you don't know courage when you see it. Courage is staying on the job after the gaff has been socked into your immortal soul up to the barb and churned about. You think it is a matter of blood and a heap of steaming bowels and the ground torn up. You ought to see a field trial We're going to one within the next two months in which a certain bird dog's going to run that can't learn courage from anybody on earth but the French Blue Devils. Go along?"

Rabbits!

(That doesn't look right. These publishers don't
seem to realize the kind of type you need to tell
about a bird dog cursed with the curse of chasing
fur. You're not allowed to swear, you know.)

RABBITS!!! (That's better.)

Dan Thorplay pulled the throttle open. Dan, un-
restrained by any censorship, cursed the entire bunny
family from ears to tail and back, a hundred and
five round trips, and never used the same word twice.
Dan is the champion intercollegiate sulphur slinger of
the state of Texas, and he needed every word in his
vocabulary.

Dan sat on the topside of his horse, on a long neck
of land that ran out into the blue water of Sam
Houston Inlet, and watched El Paso Don depart.
Ten inches in front of Don's fine nose a cotton button
bounced; and Don, who hunted birds as silently as a
spectre, was telling the world that he was North
America's premier beagle hound, and that this was
his day to yell. Gosh, what a voice! From a mile
down the long neck of land it came singing back to
Dan the old, old story that bird work was over for the
day.

Dan heaved a sigh. Dan had fired every shot in
the locker. All the standard methods for breaking a
bird dog of chasing fur had failed against the iron-
hearted obstinacy and the invincible spirit of El Paso
Don. Dan loved him for that very stubbornness.

And Dan, seeing that the big pointer had the bottom to stand punishment without losing fire, let the strapping fellow have the works; all of the old and much of the new. The pity of it was that Don was a bird dog, backwards and frontwards, up and down, inside and out and cater-cornered. Less than two years old, he used the wind like a veteran. Months of rabbit running with Ephraim Joppey's hounds had given him the wind and endurance of a fox hunter. His range was limitless.

But he didn't run all to heels—brains to match. Don knew his birds. Fields in the morning, cover at noon, streams in the hot dry hours, sunny and sheltered hillsides on cold, windy days. Don knew where to look for them, and when.

Dan had tried him out on a couple of smaller local trials. He covered his courses with a speed in his loose limbs and a gaiety in his high head and merry tail to make bird men weep for joy. The whistle would turn him about full tilt and have him dashing away on the other tack in a quarter second. He was one of those rare pups that never get so wrapped up in their hunting that they forget they are working for the boss. He looked back every once in a while, and the wave of a hat or hand would tell him what to do, and he'd do it—unless he happened to be on birds, and then two five-ton trucks and Brown's mule couldn't swerve him. Then there showed up the stubborn will of him. Whistle or word or gesture? What about 'em if a fellow's nose said birds? And what

a nose! Full-surging galloper one second, image the
next, with the game maybe two hundred yards up-
wind. The utter confidence! A thing to warm the
last drop of blood in your frozen finger tips. One
hundred and ninety of that two hundred yards at a
trot. The last ten at a walk. Drawing, they name it
—short for drawing up. When Don, with a fine dis-
regard for orders, drew on game old dog men swore
at one another happily. A sight to fill the eye; the
superb galloping sinews sliding, visible, under their
smooth, thin jacket; the sudden easing of the moun-
tain-torrent leap of them to the steady flow of trot
and cautious walk; their sudden turning solid.

"Point judges!"

There he is! Eagerness, poise, confidence, beauty,
perfection. Danny walks up. The tall weeds rattle
at the handler's step. The gallery is open-mouthed,
awaiting the low premonitory cluck, cluck, cluck and
burst of whirring wings. Dan kicks the clump of
chaparral that Don is holding, and sweet Saint Peter
be our aid in time of trouble,—

RABBITS!!!!

Judges and fellow men, the stuff is off. El Paso
Don has called it a day on birds, and giving tongue like
a muley cow he has taken Mister Bunny out of sight
over the far horizon on his last long race. Some time
El Paso Don will come back to get his tanning; some
time about nightfall, with fur in his eyeteeth. But
as far as this particular heat is concerned, the stuff,
as has been stated, is all off.

There are times when a dog has got to be punished so that he's hurt—not injured, hurt—the amount of chastising to be gauged very carefully to the dog's ability to absorb it. El Paso Don's capacity in that particular was unlimited, and Dan let him have it. Dan paddled him till the dog whip frayed. Dan hunted him on a long check cord, and when a jack jumped out let the pup go wildly to the end of the rope, and then with a warning "Hi!" brought him up time and again in a somersault that would have broken a less sturdy dog in half. Dan had knocked over dozens of rabbits in front of the pup and had hammered him with the dead animals until that dog was red from ears to tail and there wasn't left a whole bone in the carcass. Dan had tied pair after pair of dead cotton-tails about the pointer's neck and left them there till the dog worried himself to bones trying to get them off, and until Don's presence would have made you swear that the Bolshevik army was close at hand.

Dan had even tried shooting the dog instead of the bunny when Don hopped to a fur chase. But all Dan got out of that was the job of picking bird shot out of the pointer's rump.

To use Dan's own words, he abused that puppy something heinous, which was Dan's way of saying that the next step in his effort to break that dog would really be abuse; some punishment—and Dan knew all the dog butcher's methods—that would do the trick all right but might break his body or his spirit; which was equivalent to saying that Dan was ready to quit.

Dan Thorplay would a thousand times over rather see a dog with a fault or two and a high courage and gay hunting spirit than a faultless dog, cringing and lacking all initiative, looking always to his handler for instructions. And besides, Dan Thorplay still has his first dog to abuse.

Dan sat his horse and sprayed strong language all over that long neck of land down which the pointer dog had disappeared. Dan's heart was sick. The South-west trials a week away; a winner in his very hands, and that winner a rabbit runner beyond all human hope of breaking. A pointer puppy out of old Doctor's Girl. Doc Holden's pointer dog. Doc Holden's daughter's pointer dog. Dan took a breath.

By the great nine-finned buck shad, he wouldn't quit until the very day of the trial. There surely must be some way; and Dan headed his pony down the long peninsula in the direction Don had taken his rabbit.

There was a way. There generally is. Stick with 'im, Dan.

Back in the mainland, just where the long peninsula starts, there stood a prairie farmer's rambling group of buildings. The farmer had a boy—a more or less regular boy, who, early on this particular morning, had set out into the long dry grass with a double rabbit trap. Down the peninsula half a mile, at a likely spot, the boy sprung apart the two little pairs of jaws, which were fastened to the opposite ends of a three-foot length of light chain, put a tempting carrot in each trap, drove a thin stake in the ground, looped a half hitch in the middle of the chain and, dropping the circle over the top of the stake, departed on other business, visions of rabbit pie cheering his daily chores.

A few hours later, Long Ears, smelling the carrot, took a chance, with the result that one pair of light steel jaws snapped together on his outstretched neck, bringing a promising young career to an untimely but merciful end. Then the wind changed, and with the shifting of the breeze the farmer boy's daddy steps into this narrative for a second and sets fire to the dry grass on the gulf side of his place, so that the conflagration may carry down that long, uninhabited peninsula to the inlet, and there die out, freeing his house and barn from a menace that had worried him through a long spell of steady sea winds.

Dan Thorplay saw the fire coming. There were two things to do: Ride his horse out into the bay or make a back fire. Dan thought of the many little living things that would be caught between those two fires and his face grew very thoughtful. But there was the chance of miring his pony in the treacherous shore mud. Dan scratched his head; then had another thought, swung down, scratched a match and touched off the grass; and then walked slowly along, carefully trampling out the little flames which tried to travel down the peninsula with the wind. Don was down there on the point some place.

Only Don wasn't. Don had long since nabbed his game; but bird work being over for the day he had long since, ranging silently, passed within a stone's throw of Dan, and, hidden by the long buffalo grass, gone his way up toward the mainland in search of new bunny worlds to conquer. As he approached the mainland end of the peninsula a peculiar and alarming odour met him. He put up his head and tested the wind. Something was not quite right. Uneasiness stirred the pointer's heart. He stood in indecision and looked back toward the place where he had seen Dan Thorplay last. The bitter taint in the air grew stronger. Better to go right back to that stern but kindly man and get that tanning over. That man would know what to do about this menacing smell at any rate. A splendid fellow to go to when a dog was in trouble; Don had found that out. So he turned about and started. But as he took his first step another scent, delicious, irresistible, blotting out the message of danger carried by that other odour, turned him solid. Not quite the thing that started in his heart that lust for the chase that no punishment had as yet been able to quell. Here was only the joy of eating warm meat from which the life had only lately gone, for Don's nose told him that this particular rabbit was dead—a matter for investigation anyhow. So without further caution Don broke his point and stepped boldly into the clump of wild grass from which that scent came pouring, as visible to his nose as smoke from a smudge fire would be to human eyes. Snap!

A grass fire burning into the wind and one carried

before it are two different things. The former travels slowly along, going from blade to blade in a quiet and orderly progression. Depending upon the violence of the wind, a man or horse might walk through it unharmed. But the devil that capers his *danse maçabre* at the head of the wind is a devourer. Man and beast throw off incumbrances and flee. Gopher and snake, bunny and coyote, grouse and hawk, forgetting which is food and which is feeder, join in a wild and desperate torrent of flight, and when fire and back fire meet, it often happens that only those creatures that have wings escape.

Don had 'em. No condor ever had anything on Don when it came to wings. Pegasus was a selling plater compared with that pointer dog as he came down the old home stretch with that wind-blown fire scorching his tail. Snapped fast to his right forepaw was a rabbit trap, and fast to that, by a light three-foot chain, was another trap, and in that a stone-dead bunny that leaped at Don's side in unbeatable bounds; that jumped on Don's back with a clatter of jingling chain and the bruise of tempered steel; that flung itself under Don's flying feet, tripping him up and throwing him sprawling time and again so that the snarling fire fiend in his rear gained on the frantic dog until he felt the devil's breath on his very rump. Pain as of hell racked and tore at the trapped forefoot at every leap; but Don stuck to his knitting and laid himself out with a will that soon wore off the last tuft of fur from the dead bunny's hide; and he hesitated not in thought or deed when the back fire crept up to head him off. Mouth tilted high to the smoky and merciless sky above him, yelling his terror at the menace of fiery dissolution, Don set all his canvas before the gale and tore straight into the lesser fire to escape the goblin who held that pan of red coals under his tail. Hot cinders ate through the thick pads of his paws and burned them raw. That leaping, clanking fiend at his side jumped under his feet again and threw him, delicate nose first, into the embers of the still-glowing grass. The hair on his thin silk jacket smouldered and smoked; but that only made him open his throttle wider, and leaping up he passed Dan Thorplay, going a hundred miles an hour and hallooing bloody murder at every jump, no more coat on his sides than a Mexican hairless dog, the very old sizzling devil from hell himself behind him and ahead of him and on top of him and under him; a devil that tore at one chewed forefoot with the pitchfork of the damned; that leaped on him and pounded him wild with hammers of steel; that tangled his tottering legs with chains of purgatory and flung him down time and again and time and again, jarred and suffocated and frenziedly struggling on to the grilling earth. A hob-goblin from the very bottom of bottomless Sheol, in the shape of one of that fiendish race of ravening quadrupeds that are known to the world as rabbits!

Horses and dogs and men. Improve on that combination in restraint of indoor blues if you can. Cow ponies, bird dogs, field-trial bugs. The longer you size it up, the better these Southwest Trials look. An ostaperious institution. A very wholesome triangle for any typewriter to tackle after the host of rather smelly triangles that typewriters have been forced to cook and serve up under folks' noses right along. Pintos and pups and pants. Madge Holden? Present. Riding pants.

Riding pants are, or is, as the case may be, a rigid and inflexible stipulation that the Southwest Trials impose upon mere femininity if it attempts to intrude upon these masculine ceremonies. Riding pants,— not knickers. Knickers in man or woman, dear my lord, are not the immediate jewel of our soul. Man, unassisted, can by these atrocities bring enough heartache into the world. The ladies, by sincere and conscientious effort could, no doubt, find other raiment even more hideous; if that's the object. If mere bifurcation is the end in view then let us have, by all means, niftiness therewith. Now, riding breeches,— Well, the Southwest Field Trials welcomes feminine intrusion thus bedight. And, come to think of it, it might be difficult to name a gathering of men that would class Madge Holden as an intrusion. Looking at Madge, you thought at once of next year's models, which are said to embody features superior to anything that has previously been turned out. Very attractive colour scheme, sleekest upholstery you ever saw, sport model, racing chassis, stream lines. Gosh! What to do? Curse out those trim tan riding boots for hiding such a pair of ankles or bless them for revealing that glimpse of dizzying knee curves between their tops and the point where those humdingerous breeches started to swing to a half-hiding, half-revealing fulness? A long-skirted riding coat fitted her slender body to the point where men can be no longer held responsible. And she didn't wear a dinny—not by a jugful of what you would most desire to have the jug full of, she didn't wear no whamdasted fried egg of a stiff riding hat, not in this little literary misfit. She wore a jockey cap, if you want to know it. And if you ever saw hazel eyes with lovely unplucked brows, and a nose too thoroughbred to be stub and too curly—if you know what I mean—to be snobbish, and a scarlet mouth, and so forth and so on, peeping out from under the jaunty peak of a jockey cap; and a swirl of cropped hair with the sheen and colour of chestnuts in a newly opened burr spraying thickly out from under its edges, you'll excuse the present detour. Sometimes the scenery off to the left looks so blamed good that you just can't keep the old peanut roaster on the main road.

Dog men looked at Madge Holden and forgot to talk dog, and to set forth a higher encomium than that a man would have to be considerable encomer.

Shirleigh Welles, whom, like the poor, we have always with us, looked at Madge and swore by every dollar in the family coffers that that delicious morsel should be his.

Dan Thorplay looked at her and took a reverent breath, and for the first time in his life realized what his dad had been getting at when he hammered into Dan from boyhood up the fact that the wild oat is a nauseating and unnecessary weed without a drop of fighting sap in it from its slime-covered roots to its rancid and sickly flower.

El Paso Don looked at his mistress and said to himself that no gauze-bandaged, canvas-booted, strangely lifeless right forefoot would keep him from finding every blasted feather in southwestern U. S. A. if that thing had to be done to win for her. And as he looked up at her, trembling with eagerness to be sent out, the head judge spoke:

"Next brace El Paso Don and Morning Star, Gentlemen, put down your animals. Ready? Let's see 'em!"

Before the pair of straining dogs illimitable space stretched out; level to the eye, but really an endless spread of wide, low, flat-topped rises with shallow valleys in between; the billows and wave troughs of this mighty sea of grass land. In that vast game field dwelt old feather-neck in hundreds and in thousands. Sly mother birds with many a bag of tricks for use in the protection of their coveys. Wily and strong polygamous old roosters who could scuttle from sage to chaparral, from buffalo clump to mesquite, with a speed and cunning that baffle the wisest of noses.

Undaunted by the endless prairie land before them, the two young derbies swung up into the wind like all-age veterans and tore out to cover it. The day was young; birds moving about to feed; scent strong. Full tilt the slim red lady froze.

"Over there," her long nose said. "There in that clump of wild grass." And El Paso Don, his bandage not yet loosened, slid on his tail ten yards behind her, backing perfectly.

"You said a noseful, lady," said Don's stand, checking her to three decimal places. "Over there in that clump of wild grass is where they are!"

Morning Star's handler, a lanky, red-cheek-boned, sandy-haired young fellow, rode close up to his dog and swung down.

"Let's see your game," the judge said.

The long-legged man waded into the wild grass.

Cluck, cluck. Whirr, whirr, whirr, whirr! They were gone, four feathered missiles thrown full speed out of some unseen catapult. The dogs stood staunch and watched with eager eyes, and then at a word leaped on toward the little gully where their keen sight had marked down the soaring end of the scattered flight.

For an hour those two pups fought it out, back and forth in long zigzags across the course of the judges and handlers and the mounted gallery. An hour of dashing casts, half mile to right and back, half mile to left and back. An hour of top-speed galloping, of sudden stands, of instantaneous backs, of brainy obedience to whistle and gesture; an hour of bird work so uncanny that old circuit trailers gasped and pinched themselves to make sure that it wasn't an all-age running they were looking at instead of a derby race—a match for less-than-two-year-olds.

The bandage on Don's maimed foot grew red. Men wondered why, doglike, he didn't sit down and tear that hindering boot to pieces. Men didn't know that Dan Thorplay had sat up with the dog the whole of the previous night to prevent that very thing, soaking that unhealed foot, from which so short a time ago he had amputated two smashed toes, with a weak cocaine solution until at last Don had no feeling in the paw at all.

So, with his bandage dripping red, Don kept at it, trying his mightiest to run past that red wraith ahead, but failing because of a cursed wooden stump of a leg that somehow would not take perfectly the calls for speed that his will sent down to it. But for his marvellous nose he would have lost the heat. But many a time, ten yards behind the Irish setter, he would flash to a stand a tenth of a second before she did as the scent of game told his wizard nostrils the story that she also caught a fractional second late. And once or twice, in her twin-six going across the wind, her speed carried her clean past a spot where Don, a jump or two behind, pulled up short, let the Irish lady run, whirled, drew trotting up the breeze, walked, froze and nailed the game she had missed.

"Take up your livestock, gentlemen!"

An hour? Sure, an hour!

"The next brace—"

'—an hour of top speed galloping, of sudden stands,
f instantaneous backs.'

But Dan Thorplay never heard their names. He flung an arm about his bloody-footed pup and loped for the dog wagon. With hasty knife he slit off the foul bandage. Madge Holden gave a little cry and turned glistening eyes to her father.

"Thank heaven, dad, it's over!"

"I only wish it were!" the handler muttered, and, soaking his cotton wad in the cocaine, again applied it to the pitiful foot. Don whimpered.

"I saw my dog, Brass Knuckles, have his leg crunched clear off by Mike Mullany's bitch, Death Grip, in the pit one night, but I've yet to hear my first whimper come off of the tan-bark!"

Madge Holden's breast leaped with a sharp intake of breath as she shuddered back against her father's side.

Dan Thorplay whirled about, handing a mangled paw and a dripping cotton wad to Doc.

"Listen, Apollo Belvedere!" snapped the handler, shooting a quick glance of appraisal over the broad, immaculate young giant who had just finished speaking. "Unless you want the fun of licking a man who's giving you seventy-five pounds, ring side, don't make another crack like that. That kind of stuff is fit for bar talk, not for ladies. And besides, that pointer dog isn't squealing. He just heard the judge say 'Let go!' and he weeps because he can't go along and hunt that leg off up to the elbow."

Mr. Welles, assuming his most contumelious air, stared past Dan Thorplay as though that gentleman did not exist. Dan's face grew hot. He walked up to Mr. Welles until his chest was brushing against the middle buttons of Shirleigh's waistcoat.

"Hey, Tarzan of the Apes," Dan called up, "look down here before I kick you in the shins!"

At this threat to his dignity Shirleigh glanced downward in great surprise at finding himself addressed by one to whom he had not yet been properly introduced.

"Maybe you can get away with this supercilious-nabob stuff back home in little old New York," Dan told him, "but out here there are ways to insult a man without knocking him down or saying that his dog lacks guts; so if you don't quit looking past me like you were wearing a piece of Limburger cheese for a scarfpin you're likely to turn this dog race in to a man race, with me in the lead. But I'm telling you now, you'll never catch me, for I'll be running on the bare ground, and you'll be running through spit-out teeth up to your knees!"

Shirleigh glared over his barrel chest at Dan, and turning contemptuously on his heel walked over to the little car where Morning Star, wrapped in a light blanket, lay snuggled on the lap of her lanky red-cheek-boned handler.

When Shirleigh Wells desired to humiliate some one his first care was to rally a good old gang of the family dollars about him. With these to back him he had wrought the discomfiture of many a better man than himself, and along these lines of attack he proceeded now. Shirleigh had a scheme. The old hatrack was functioning. Money and brains; great combination.

"I shoot over Irish setters," said Shirleigh to the lanky man, "and I know that their wonderful work to the gun has kept them with the hunters; but I was always sure that the Irishmen could put it across at the races if a good trial man took hold of them. I want to congratulate you."

Undreamed-of diplomacy. Shirleigh's cylinder block was hitting on six all right. Such a start properly followed, and the lanky man was his friend for life.

"What's her breeding?" asked Shirleigh next.

Mr. Welles was inspired, absolutely. There followed a flow of pedigree talk for half an hour that meant as much to Welles as that much Choctaw; but he let the man rave back generation after generation, as dog men will, until he had crossed the sea and was prowling about in pagan Ireland for this Star dog's first forbears. But at last he made the mental round trip, landing in southwestern U. S. A., and when he came up for air Mr. Welles played the next card in the game.

"What's the chance that the judges will want to see your bitch and the pointer again?"

"Hundred-to-one shot," the setter man came back decisively. "That heat was easy the class race of the morning, and a dead heat if ever I saw one."

Things were working out—a chance to beat this fellow Thorplay at his own game. He would tell

Shirleigh Welles what was proper and what improper talk before a lady? Shirleigh took the plunge.

"I could put unlimited cash into a venture to put Irish setters into the field trials, and I'd like to do it. They tell me this little bitch is yours. How much would she set me back if I wanted to start such a venture with her to head my kennels and you my manager?

Did that lanky boy fall? With a life's ambition within his grasp? You inform 'em!

"By the way," said Shirleigh, putting the cap back on his fountain pen, "I've heard a lot of whispered talk in the gallery about rabbits to-day. Is it true that the pointer isn't fur proof?"

A chuckle.

"Fur proof? Say, listen, Mr. Welles! I've been praying for rabbits all morning. The devil knows where the jacks are keeping themselves. Another day and they'd be bouncing about all over the place. I've been down on my knees for one—just one. Gimme that, O Lord, and I see the end of a perfect day, with that pointer's tail a-waving us all good-by as he and his friends head for the border. Fur proof?" And he fairly glowed with hope.

His new employer nodded wisely once or twice, and leaving him glowing went over to a long, low, scarlet roadster, and smiling like a cat on a robin's trail kicked her off, swapped ends and stormed away in the direction of the headquarters town a few miles back.

Billy Rees was talking; than whom, when it comes to sportsmanship, squareness, loving dogs and judging field trials, there is no than-whomer gentleman in America. When Billy Rees addressed a field-trial crowd he always started off with the word "gentlemen." Billy had explained one time that there was no risk of a mistake in using the word at such gatherings. To make use of his own very expressive adverb, a person who unsloppily loved a dog couldn't possibly fail in gentleness, no matter how much man he happened to be.

"Gentlemen," said Billy Rees, "and I think that title may, without offence to any one, be made to include Miss Holden, there will be one second-series race today. The judges agree that the first running of El Paso Don and Morning Star was tie, and would like to see those pups again."

The two dogs were brought forward, both straining eagerly; Morning Star's glorious red coat gleaming like a meteor; Don limping ever so little from the tightness of his new bandages.

"Gentlemen," said Billy Rees, "I look for history. Put down your bird dogs. Are you ready?"

"Not quite." There was menace in the words; menace in the smooth, suave, domineering voice that spoke them. Something warned that Billy Rees was right. Dog history was in the making. "Is there not a rule," the arrogant voice went on, "against the use of stimulants or sedatives of any kind to dope a dog at trials?"

Rees nodded, a frowning comprehension dawning back of his steel-rimmed spectacles.

"I'll ask you to examine the pointer's bandages then."

Dan Thorplay doubled up a fist and looked about for some one that would hold his pointer's leash. But the judge glanced his way and held up a quieting hand. Light of suppressed anger shone through the steel rings as Billy turned his headlights on the speaker.

"All the judges knew that the dog's foot was doped when he finished the first heat with his boot still on," said Rees to Shirleigh quietly.

"Is there some good reason, then, for discriminating in favour of the pointer?" asked Welles insolently.

"It happens," answered Billy Rees, his whole countenance now dark with the effort to control his temper, "that we have asked the setter's owner if he objects to the cocaine on the pointer's bandage."

"Perhaps you have asked the setter's handler," spoke up Welles, playing his trump card with unbearable loftiness, "but you haven't asked her owner."

"Oh, yes, you have, judge!" came a voice with such a puncturing emphasis that Shirleigh's inflated chest fell like the crop of a pouter pigeon; and Andy Mac-Andrews pulled Morning Star over toward the judge, extracting a narrow slip of paper from his shirt pocket as he came.

"Sometimes," quoth Andy, "a check makes a mighty bum receipt, especially when one party to a transaction takes special precautions that there are no witnesses about." The sandy-haired man had been tearing up the slip of paper as he spoke. With a flip of his hand he tossed a little snowstorm into the air. "This setter is my dog," he added, "and I'd like to see anything from six feet one on up try to get her away from me. The pointer runs as is."

"Judge," said Dan Thorplay, "I'd like to bandage dry. Can you hold this heat up for five minutes?"

Billy Rees stared at Dan a moment. Then he smiled his famous smile and put a hand on Dan's shoulder.

"There's only one kind of animal I like better than a fighting fool of a dog, and that's a fighting fool of a man. I'd hold this heat up five minutes or five hours for either one. But when that foot hurts, Dan, he's going to tear that bandage off, and you know what that means."

"We'll take a chance," Dan made answer. "Got to. There's a pit-dog murderer here today who thinks that this Don pup won't run if his foot starts to hurt, when I know that the only way to keep that animal from hunting birds is to lock his nose up in a safe-deposit vault. If pointer dogs are yellow, then pointer men are yellow—and pointer women. For the sake of bird dogs and bird-dog folks I'd like to bandage dry."

Dan looked at Dr. Amos Holden, who moved his head ever so slightly. Dan knelt beside El Paso Don and took the dog's right paw on his thigh. Then as he

reached for his pocketknife he turned his eyes inquiringly to the girl at Holden's side. Impulsively
she stepped toward the two, and sinking to a crouch
flung a swift arm about the pointer's neck.

"We bandage dry," she said.

The day had passed its height only a little while
before. The air was still and hot. The sun beat.
Birds were still. Scent poor. Fortune had set in
hard against the pointer, for the prairie that had
teemed with chicken but a few hours before, now
seemed tenantless. Search as they might, the two
dogs did not make a find during the first half hour.
Dan Thorplay cursed. Speed, speed, speed! That
was the thing that was going to win this race. Cover
the ground! Eat up the country! Go! Not a
feather to stop that endless galloping; and the red
dog always a bit ahead, and during the last few minutes steadily gaining. At last, with the setter leading
by a dozen leaps, the pointer seemed to lose heart.
He slowed up, trotted for a little with a decided limp,
sat down. The judges looked at each other. The
reluctant shaking of their heads as they talked quietly
together said plainer than any words that a longer
running seemed both unnecessary and cruel. Dan
Thorplay drew a tired breath. Shirleigh Welles, deep
in his scarlet roadster, roared his idling motor insolently. The superior disdain on his classic features
was not half so maddening as that preliminary, mock-
ing, cut-out laughter. For him the race was over.

Bird-dog courage? Even the burly power-proud engine up ahead of him shouted unmuffled and contemptuous glee; and Shirleigh started to twist his steering wheel, about to shake from his tires the dust of such a pitiful exhibition of pluck.

And then on a sudden the unsportsmanlike ho-ho-ing of that big bully of an engine was drowned out and cut short by the yell that tore up out of Dan Thorplay's exultant throat, for with one single mighty yank of his long fangs El Paso Don had ripped that crippling canvas boot apart. Another slash or two and the air was filled with bloody lint. That foot had started to hurt. The effects of that long doping had started to wear away. Off she came. Of course it hurt. What of it? At least a dog now knew that he had a foot at the end of that long-time numb right foreleg. At least that foot was free. Don rose. Don shook himself as though just landing from a far, hard swim. The muscles rippled under his thin coat, each hard-trained thew in view. Speed, eh?

Dogs for uncounted years have carried the name of Don. Mutts have borne it. Mongrels innumerable have sported it. Bulldog and mastiff; Scotty and sealyham; collie and black and tan have claimed it. But it's a pointer name. Don! Master, nobleman, aristocrat in the richest value of the word; no title but for the strongest and the finest; a name honoured by many a modern pointer dog's ancestors, the staid and staunch and dignified old *punteros* that stood their birds long centuries ago for their masters of that day, the proud young Dons of ancient Spain.

At last that cursed ribbon of rags that kept a fellow's pastern sinews stiff and inflexible was off. Don looked about. Far out to the left he saw Star ranging at her endless gallop, endlessly searching for those devilish birds. The red lady was right. There were birds somewhere. Carry your nose on wide enough range, cover the country. Sooner or later that nose will spot 'em. Well, let's go! And Don, free of that crippling bandage, gathered together his long clean thews, gave one deep bark of delight, made a great leap and was off.

Far off to the south the setter swung about to her handler's whistle, but to the wonder of the gallery Don did not turn when she came sailing past. Don finished his cast. Don did not trust that setter's nose, and with the mighty desire within his heart to turn and race her Don answered the mightier desire to do a good and honest piece of work, and he went on, searching the ground that the setter had just hunted, until Dan Thorplay's whistle turned him also. And then El Paso Don, the son of Doctor's Girl, laid his chest to the ground, called for the mighty heart that hammered inside his ribs to stick and shook loose the last links of his going. Old dog men, watching, tried to talk to each other about this thing that they saw before them, but finding they couldn't, pounded each other on the back.

Stiff-necked Shirleigh, austere Shirleigh, self-engrossed Shirleigh, deep in his scarlet roadster, missed it all, of course. The only thing he saw, to his chagrin, was a bloody-footed dog pulling up jump by jump on a red streak just ahead, running that red streak nose and nose, and at last, to the yell of a crazy gallery, leaping into the lead. Shirleigh missed, as the self-centred always miss, the thing that counts, the beautiful thing, the very thing in fact that Shirleigh claimed to be looking for; that undefeatable something that beats in the hearts of champions, two legged and four; the nerve to play, come suffering or whatever, the final card; to do, come hell or high water, that very last heartbreaking level damnedest than which no golden-haloed angel in heaven can do more.

Heels, eh? All right then, heels it is! Range—killing range! Wide birdless cast after wide birdless cast! The two dogs' tongues hung out. No pause for water. By theory the pointer should have reaped an advantage there long before this. By theory the long-haired setter should have felt that scorching sun and stopped for a drink long since. But dogs like Morning Star follow no theories. Dogs like Morning Star hunt birds, and hunt and hunt, and the devil fly away with theories. So it was that El Paso found no help in theories that day. The only help for El Paso Don lay in El Paso Don, and the fates were against him. His marvellous nose gave him no aid in this bird-barren land. Even his bird-wise brain stood him in no stead whatever. Your help, El Paso Don, lies in your mighty muscles and in the stout pointer heart that hammers within you. And dog men, watching him—watching the thing that Welles was missing, quit thumping each other on the back and stood in silence; a silence broken only by their own loud breathing.

Dog men know that the endurance runners take their propulsion from the shoulder; that for the long galloping of a bird-finding race no dog is built to stand the shock of body weight that back-leg springing hurls down upon shoulders and pasterns. The greyhound, with his form pared down to gauntness, mere lungs and a heart on mighty muscled legs, the last ounce of excess weight bred off his body by centuries of selection, is made to stand the terrific speed shocks of back-leg springing that is necessary for the pursuer of game by eye; for the long-sustained sprint with which the sight hunter must get his quarry. But the scent hunter, with his staying gallop, leaps from the shoulder, with his back legs picked up beneath him except when put down to carry his hind parts along. The hind leg spring is only for leaping obstacles, or for maximum speed in the sprint. And yet for a full and punishing half hour old bird men watched with deep-breathing lungs and fast-beating hearts as El Paso Don hurled the weight of his big body mercilessly down onto that mangled forefoot with the cruel sprinting gallop that he found must be used to put him on the outside of Morning Star and keep him there.

No birds? Birds, curse their wily little hearts, were somewhere! And birds he would dig up out of

that prairie, and dig them up ahead of that setter girl
if it took him to Mexico. That bandage was gone.
Now a fellow could run. Now a fellow knew that he
had a foot, even though every time he put it down
he had the bad luck to land it on a long, sharp, white-
hot pitchfork tine.

At least that right foreleg ended no longer in lifeless nothingness in which a dog could place no confidence whatever. No longer need a fellow hesitate
to fling his weight forward, white-hot pitchfork tines
or not, for at least a flesh-and-blood paw was there
to take the shock. And so for a little while, a tortured but glorious little while, that pointer pup kept on
the outside of the merciless, birdless running.

But larger and larger blood daubs were marking his
every leap, and the liver-spotted white of his right
side changed colour as though some thick, dripping
brush had splashed him over with bright vermilion.

"See that dog race?" asked Doc Holden. His voice
was the least bit tense as he leaned across the door
of the scarlet roadster and asked the question.
"There's a pointer dog on a job of work out there.
He's only a pup, and he's not having any fun. See
that low tail? The sport has long since gone out of
that pointer's hunting. He's a sick pointer dog.
Torture has hold of him. Hell pains shoot from that
foot all over his body at every jump. But watch
when that setter pulls out ahead of him. There!
See his big thighs smashing his body down onto that
messed-up foot. There's a dog in travail, Welles.

But there's birds out there somewhere, and that pointer dog's going to find them; mind what I tell you, Welles. That's his job. That's his work. I don't believe you know what you're watching, Welles; but take a good look. It's courage!"

But now a presence other than torture took hold of El Paso Don; a thing with sagging rags for sinews and ropes for bones and leaden weights for feet; a grim and ghastly spectre that came up with him and looked with pouched and sallow-ringed eyes into his own and laid thin, listless hands upon him. Don leaped with fright. Don feared this slack-kneed, tottering, vermin-crusted thing. It wasn't death. Don hated death; would fight it savagely to the last breath and heartbeat when it came. But he wasn't afraid of it. Don was a pointer dog. This thing was Fatigue. Don had never known it before. Weariness to the point of agony he had known; but weariness a dog could fling off by a great trying; and fling off again and again and again. But leap as he might, spring as he would, Don could not tear free of the clutch of those listless, sticky, down-bearing, persistent hands.

Deep in Don's wounded foot a little artery had come open and a tiny fountain spurted in that haggled paw at every pulse. The flood that jumped through Don's elastic veins was ebbing. The canals that carried away the poisons of wear and tear were running low, and instead of being burned up in the keen fire of his lungs venomous toxins now were lying about thick in his sickening body, awaiting removal. Blood was the thing he needed—even a good big squirt of warm salt solution. Something, anything, to pick up and carry to his lungs those clogging motes with which that languid fiend with the sticky hands was choking him. Struggle and gallop, he could not shake off those terrible fingers. Heart thumping bravely with effort to pump that diminishing flow of red life out to the dying tissues, he tried, tried, tried, till the hearts of the judges melted, to catch that red lady who now was hopelessly far in the lead.

"Gentlemen, call in your dogs!"

Two whistles sounded. Two dogs whirled. Two tired puppies, one a-stagger from blood loss, started their race back to their handlers. The lash of losing somehow put a moment of strength into the pointer's legs as the Irish lady passed him on the way in. For a leap or two he kept pace with her. Then with his tongue lolling far, eyes dull, tail limp, but with the good old will to win and the rarer will in this day and generation to do the best day's work within him, driving the blood-spattered, pain-racked body of him to its last game effort, he saw the red girl leave him. One of the scrawny hands that pulled down on his hips reached forward and shut the light out of his eyes. Just as the dimness came he saw the Irish girl a hundred feet ahead rise in the air, and with a grand free leap clear a little drainage hollow close before the judges. There was now no chance to win back to the handlers first. That setter girl was already stretched on soft straw under the soothing hands of those she loved. No chance to win. But by the great god of dogs there was the chance to finish this race like a pointer. So, judging the distance he had to go, with eyes entirely blind with ache and agony, El Paso Don staggered up to the edge of the drainage ditch and flung himself out in the direction of the far bank. Those slimy fingers were still across his eyes. But try as that feeble clinging fiend might try, those cold dead fingers could reach no farther forward. For of all the processes that spelled life in that once brilliantly living and sparkling body, one would continue to function till the last heart throb died away.

Halfway across the little swale, legs limp and pendulous, head down, tail down, tongue lolling; fainting in very midair, crashing to senselessness into the wet, rank grass, that blind dog saw again; saw twenty times as clearly as ever the eyes of you or me will see a thing this side the grave. From the still air an invisible hand reached out and took El Paso Don by the long, square muzzle; a hand that brushed aside the dreadful fingers of fatigue and snapped the dog about end for end and dropped him onto the swampy bottom of that little swale, quivering, tense, life charged. The long clean neck stretched forward. The great bow of his stifles bent in deep-curved arc ready for pouncing into that clump of furze over which the fast-going Morning Star had leaped to defeat a second or so before. Needle tail stiffly level hunting lust bright in those eyes again, actually feeling the air with soft little nostril caresses, Don looked straight through that cover with a vision unknown and mysterious to man, and nailed 'em tight to the mast.

The blood ran off that butchered, upheld foot, not in drops but steadily, in a little stream that spurted at regular intervals like a tiny fountain. A red stain spread in a puddle of water beneath him, and spread and spread. What of it? Don, blessed old fire-eating Castilian Don—he had 'em!

The field-trial party rode up to gaze, and a long scarlet roadster rolled to the edge of the swale along with the cavalcade. Dan Thorplay was the only one who saw the shameful thing. Until his dog is taken up a handler is supposed to be a sort of combination Argus and Sherlock Holmes; nothing is supposed to get away from him. Dan Thorplay is a dog handler with a hundred and nine more eyes than the specifications call for. So it happened that while the gallery watched Dan's dog, Dan, out of the corner of one of his extra eyes, saw a door open in the side of that scarlet roadster and caught the flip of a bag.

"Careful!" said Dan.

Under El Paso Don's very nose the cotton ball whisked. The gallery groaned in horror at such an unspeakable piece of misfortune. The gallery knew all about El Paso Don and rabbits. So did Dan Thorplay. But Dan didn't groan. Dan grinned, a merry, gleeful, gloating grin. And Don, the blessed pup, who knew full well that a fiery, clanking, hammering, foot-crunching, scorching devil lived under the deceitful hide of every harmless-looking bunny that infested the earth, stood like a statue and let that tuft of cotton brush his nose. Feathers—feathers, my boy, were Don's vocation; fur his most fascinating aversion.

Old steel-rimmed Billy watched the rabbit out of sight. Then he turned to Dan.

"Mr. Thorplay," he stated, "most of us folks are going to hug this day to our chests when they tuck in our cedar kimonos under our chins for the last long snooze; so we want it finished right. I've got my suspicions that you've got a bird dog down there in that swale. If so, does it so happen, by the grace of God, that you have taught him to flush on order?"

"Yes, sir," said Dan. "He's got it all."

Billy reached out a hand took a single-barreled shotgun from one of the other judges.

"Show me!" directly Billy.

"Let's see 'em, Don!" said Dan.

El Paso Don, with a single mighty effort leaped forward and crashed down headfirst, limp and helpless into the clump of furze. A mighty old cock got up with a roar of wings and tore off in strong, hard flight, and as he stuck his outstretched head into a handful of spinning bird shot, just as old Steel Specs had planned he should, El Paso Don proved that among his other virtues was staunchness to wing and shot, for without another move, just where he lay, he very quietly slipped out of a world of fatigue and torture and into another delicious one of cool and yielding straw and unbelievably sweet water for his throat and bland ointments for his hell-racked paw, and soft hands and a softer voice, and the gentle splash of feminine tears on that long wonder nose.

"Doc," said Dan Thorplay, when the things had quieted down a bit, "man to man, what's your opinion of these here things?"

Doc took a close-up, cross-eyed scrutiny, and then a long enquiring sniff at each of the two bunches of knuckles that Dan held up to him.

"The man smell is very strong on both of them," Doc stated. "Why do you ask?"

"Well," Dan replied, "I just wanted a little free medical advice. I plan rough usage for 'em shortly. Order me lilies of the valley, signifying innocence and purity, and plant me deep where the woodbine twineth and the whangdoodle whineth for its first-born. As my last act on earth I'm going over there and kiss Ethelbert on the alabaster brow with an over-hand right."

Doc Holden put a hand against Dan's chest.

"What's the brilliant thought?" asked Doc. "He's ripe for a butchering all right, but this is a field trial, not an abattoir. You can't go about swinging and jabbing and piling up stiffs like cordwood just because folks don't happen to strike your fancy. Cool off!"

"Cool off my grandmother's black cat's tail!" snapped Dan. "I saw the big he charlotte-russe eater drop that rabbit out of the door of his roadster.'

Doc opened his mouth. Then he shut it again till he got control of himself. Then he grinned as one who for many days has quietly bided his time. He led Dan off to a side. Then, covertly, he pulled his right shirt sleeve back, exposing nineteen pounds of forearm.

"Insect to insect," asked Doc, in a dirty-work-at-the-cross-roads whisper, "what do you think of that?'

Dan tried to make a dent in exhibit B.

"Cat bird!" Dan answered, sotto voce. "We'l both take a poke at him. There's plenty of him for everybody."

"Hurt Shirleigh's pride in his physical strength and you flay him and sprinkle him well with salt. Leave this to doctor," the elder man advised, and he started over to where that young giant was trying to get Madge Holden to look up from her dog.

"Come now," said Doc, "you'll give me your hand on bird-dog courage after that exhibition, won' you?"

And Shirleigh, hoping that the pretence of being a good loser might help his desperate case with the doctor's daughter, forced a stiff smile and bit—bit hard and hearty, reached out a mighty paw and, all unsuspecting, placed it in the bear trap that Doc was holding out to him.

A minute passed.

"There's a pointer puppy in the wagon there tha

deserves an apology from you, Shirleigh. Are you
man enough to make it?"

Silence.

"Oh, well!" said Doc. And remembering that
flash of cotton beneath his half-dead pointer's nose,
gave another twist to the wheel of the letter press.
Dan Thorplay watched in silence until he saw the
blood ooze out from under the polished finger nails.

Then, "Has some one a thirty-eight?" asked Dan.

Somebody, puzzled as to what was in Dan's mind
but confident that whatever course Dan pursued with
his gun would be an eminently wise one, came forward
and proffered his hardware. Dan waved a hand.

"You use it," Dan directed, watching for the tears
that presently rolled out upon the aristocratic cheeks.
"When Marmaduke the Malted-Milk Hound goes
down on a knee you shoot me. I always hankered to
die happy!"

The charming lady that Dan Thorplay and Doc
Holden watched as she sat tailor fashion on the floor
of the dog wagon was a slender lady as well. She
was made none the less charming by the fact that a
pointer dog was sleeping with his head in her lap—
and none the less slender. If she had weighed two
ounces less, this lady, she would have been thin. But
she wasn't. Five thousand reward to the man who
can point out an angle. She was slender, slim—
tenuous, maybe—low-curved, slight. Now we've got
it.

"And the form of her is slight
    As the crescent moon at night."

Who painted to order that midsummer night's word
picture of Madge Holden anyway?

"What's my chances?"

Dan Thorplay's eyes were wide with the wonder of
a world that gives a man the privilege to fight for a
thing like that.

"Fine here!"

"But with her—and a million bucks against me?"

"What chance has a golden dollar when it stacks up
against that other rare bit of mintage, a solid-gold,
scrapping-man's heart? We pause," added Doc, with
the normal man's distaste for being caught at oratory,
"for a reply."

He didn't get one. His audience in fact seemed
much preoccupied.

"Some dogs," stated the audience absently, "have
all the luck. And yet he deserves it. That pointer
pup certainly did find every last one."

Piqued at this lack of response to his eloquence
our orator frowned in high dudgeon, whatever that is

"Every last what?" he demanded.

"Prairie chicken," said Dan.

Zanoza

I

Radyikk Olnovsk unslung the long, slim horn that hung beneath the armpit of his thick hunting tunic and lifted it toward his lips. From what his experienced ears told him of the excited baying of the *guanchi,* deep in the forest back of him, he would need the help of that thick-headed Mastov Borloff, and of the great White Falcon, and of the smaller but more terrible Tersai, and of Zanoza, the sweet-hearted little bitch. Also, the Master would, of course, be with his favourite trio; and old friend knout would see to it that some kennel huntsman slept on his stomach for many a night, if the Master should miss the wild joy of coursing on this perfect morning. So Radyikk Olnovsk awkwardly pushed aside his moustache and beard with a mittened hand, and tucked his thick lips into the mouthpiece of the narrow silver arc.

The belling of the trail hounds rose. Back where the snow had been held up from the ground by the interlacing boughs overhead the short-legged *guanchi* sped along, nose to the ground, filling the awesome gloom of the vast tree-columned, snow-arched forest corridor with savage, dolourous, beautiful music.

And far ahead of them, huge, dim grey shapes slunk out of sheltering lairs and started loping easily, ahead of the pack, toward the forest edges and the open.

Thus it went always. Yet the injustice of it never soured the big hearts of the scent hunters. Each time that the pack of them was unleashed on one side of the Master's wide, dark preserve, they would start fearlessly into the dim aisles, following the quarry through the miles that finally led out on the other side of the wood, into the deep snow of the open; from which point the good old *guanchi* would flounder sturdily and hopelessly in the trail and come at last to a trampled, snow-tossed space, blood-spattered, where the long-limbed borzoi had run down the scent hound's rightful victim. But then what mattered it? Theirs was the plodder's task—performed as nobly, if not so spectacularly, as was the borzoi's. What one of these long-legged sight hunters, anyway, could have ever found a wolf in his dark forest lair? There was a task for a nose! And the good Master knew it; and was prodigal of fine, gruff words of praise and of hearty hand slaps when they came plowing and panting through the snow up to the place of the kill; and denied not even the greenest puppy, running novice with the pack, the privilege of sniffing with nose up tight against the still warm fur —that strong, soul-satisfying scent, which is the natural perfume of the domestic dog triple extracted, the infinitesimal trace of which on days-old footprints had started the glorious chase.

But now the pony of Radyikk Olnovsk started to
stamp the snow; and the three borzoi strained and
tugged at the leash in Radyikk's hand. For the long,
sad song of the *guanchi* was ringing not a verst back
in the cover. Suddenly snow scattered from the
bushes at the edge of the wood not fifty *sagenes* away.
The rough-coated pony's forelock tossed. Rasboi,
Kantovla and the little girl Saiga stretched rawhide
until it was with difficulty that the kennel man kept
his saddle. *Ai,* now! Would that thick-skulled Mastov Borloff—who, by what witchery no one knew, had
come into charge of the wolf team that had won the
Golden Trumpet at the great field trials at Valdoksiva
—would he never come dashing round that forest
angle, past which he and the Master had gone on to
the next station a half hour ago? Shall a man blow
his very lungs out through the bell of the silver horn
and still that blockhead not give heed?

The light breeze that swept the steppe was toward
Radyikk and his hounds; and it must have brought
over the snow, from beyond that woody projection, a
strong suspicion of an approaching menace. For one
huge, tan-gray shape stole out from under the snow-
covered bush, and another followed, and a third—
and a fourth, even, came into view, before the first
one of that quartet of sharp, inquiring noses turned
to sniff into the lee and discerned the danger there.

Too close now was the baying back in the trees
to seek again the cover that wolfish instinct knew
would let them elude those three long, straining hounds

that hunted by sight alone. Better to trust to a speed that had never before been matched. And the four gaunt beasts broke into the loping gallop that had run down every ill-fated creature that had ever crossed their famished way.

But now a mellow death knell blew its bell note out of a golden hunting horn after the fleeting brutes, and, rocking in his high Cossack saddle, the Master came scudding round the bend of the projecting angle of the forest with a speed that whipped out straight the gay black-and-yellow streamers from the bottom of his lance's head. And suddenly out ahead of him a black, flat shadow sped. Almost invisible in the morning sun against the snow was the white hound that cast it. Upon which, all courtesy due the Master having been observed, Radyikk cast loose his triple leash.

Now soared again that ancient Muscovite glee at hounding to the death those enemies that have been taking toll from cattle and horse and man since the first winter came down on the steppes. More feared and hated by mankind than any other wild beast is the wolf. Cowardly and brave, slinking and bold, merciless, evil, strong, terrible and wise, man has woven about his breed a legendry that is sinister and wonderful, and as ancient and universal as the legend of the Deluge; so that one studying it comes at last almost to believe that there must be some basis for it.

And so vindictive rapture surged in the heart of

Radyikk Olnovsk when Rasboi, the big brigand, struck the hindmost wolf with his shoulder and rolled him in the snow. Like light the wolf regained his feet and started on; but now the brigand leaped at his left side, just safe beyond the teeth that clicked at him over the lurching gray shoulder; and so they ran until suddenly the swift Kantovla, by a rare burst of speed, came up to the harried beast, along his right flank, and knocked him down again and got away without a scratch. So when the wolf had whirled the deadly circle of his fangs about the centre where his rump was seated in the snow and then started off again, he found a great dog running on either side of him. He flashed his fangs at right and left, but the wolfhounds simply leaped along beside him at a safe distance, too perfectly trained to attempt more than the worrying of him yet. And, at last, just as the hunted beast had settled again to his best stride, his white, snapping teeth protecting him on either side, the little girl, Saiga, mild-eyed as the doe from which she got her name, threw herself against his rump.

The doomed wolf never stood on his four paws again. Rasboi, the dashing big brigand, snapped his long jaw shut on the back of the thick-furred neck. Kantovla closed his fangs through the sinews of a foreleg. And the little girl, caring not a cleaned-off bone for the dignity of things, so long as she kept clear of the desperate, cutting fangs, fastened herself complacently at the root of the bushy tail. And the snow still sprayed and leaped like white water in a rapid when Radyikk Olnovsk came galloping up and stood, lance ready, waiting for the chance to thrust.

Thus ran the wonderful team from Radyikk Olnovsk's leash and thus pulled down their wolf gloriously. And thus sat Radyikk Olnovsk on his thick-coated Turkoman pony, breathing broad-chested breaths of the fine, frosty morning air, as he waited with his slim lance poised, gloating over one more squirming member of the accursed race that had stolen the infant son of ruddy Berthe Nicklocheva out of his very village and left her raving till her death, while they had dragged the baby to the forest and there, instead of mercifully devouring him, had suckled him on the milk of hell.

But not thus hunted the champion wolf team of all Russia. One wolf to the standard trio of two dogs and a bitch—that was perfect coursing. But three wolves now raced away into the steppe ahead of the Master's team—and those who win Golden Trumpets in this world are those who take methods approved as perfect by the years, and make them merely tools of genius to evolve better things.

Krilatka, the White Falcon, wisest and grandest borzoi of all Russia, stretching his mighty legs over a perfect coursing snow, just a trifle too deep for swiftest wolf speed, caught up soon to the hindmost of the three remaining brutes. The click of teeth, a thud of bone, a whirl of snow spray! It was as simple as that to Krilatka; and the great hound, instead of staying with the fallen wolf till Tersai, the hot-headed Tearer-to-Pieces, came to his aid, leaped on ahead after the second wolf, and soon had him also tumbling paws over head; nor stopped with him, but kept right on, without loss of a stride, until he was running just behind the big, wild leader.

Tersai, the Tearer-to-Pieces, who had not quite the speed of the White Falcon, came upon the third wolf just as he was scrambling to his feet, and upon the second in like manner, and, having knocked down both of them sprawling and snarling with a blow of his galloping shoulder, he likewise left them back of him for Zanoza and the Master to deal with; and went on ahead to help Krilatka hold the last grey devil till Mastov Borloff should come galloping up. Thus the noblest wolfing team in Russia started their bold attempt to do a thing that had been thought impossible up to that day. Despite the fine courage of the borzoi, they are not trained to try to kill, but to delay and harry the game till the arrival of the huntsman; and so are schooled to work in teams of three. Thus no one of them must close with the wolf at the end of the chase. Doubtful would be the issue for any one of the family of the Canidæ that might try conclusions single-handed with the wild progenitor of the race. Therefore, the borzoi is taught to make speed his weapon of offence, courage his shield.

But the Golden Trumpet team of Baron Ladislaus Michaelovitch, of Astronov, worked not by rules— three to a wolf—that day; thus to allow two of that hell breed to make their escape out on the wide stretches of the steppe. On every hunt that wonderful, championship team was wont to meet each new coursing situation with a new solution; and so, because they hunted with brain as well as with eye and leg and heart, they were the pride of Russia.

Krilatka, the White Falcon, had been known to disappear beyond the far white horizon leaping beside a giant wolf, and to bring him back in a vast circle, into the vision of his team mates again, at the end of a half a day, veering his prey ever to left and to left and to left, bumping cautiously, annoyingly and endlessly against his right shoulder. What stands, what angry desperate whirls avoided, what fencing, what bursts of terrible speed the silent wastes witnessed while the great hound was running fearlessly, alone, on the outside circumference of that wide, lonely, perilous circle, no one could ever know. But after many long hours the two leaping figures would reappear on the sky line; and once in the sight of the waiting team mates, to whom the scent trail he left behind meant nothing, the long chase was as good as done.

Tersai, the Tearer-to-Pieces, had won his name from a berserk hatred of the wolf breed, which raged so mightily in him that no trainer's lash had ever been able to subdue it. Through all his puppyhood, and a year beyond, he had been made to run in muzzle, in order to teach him that it was the huntsman's work to kill.

And Zanoza, the Sweetheart, added to the White

Falcon's incredibly keen eye and matchless power of flight and one hundred and twenty-five pounds of cool-headed courage, and to the terrible Tersai's brilliant and savage valour, an adroit shiftiness that made her a very marvel in the mad whirl of the kill; and brought up the sum of qualities of her team to the total which made these three long hounds the joy of coursing Russia.

But where was the little Zanoza now? What was the matter with the little Sweetheart? questioned the wise brain in Krilatka's long and beautiful skull. All was not well!

Long before the Master's pony had come up to the hindmost of the wolves, that brute, left unmolested by each of the two hounds that had knocked him over, and untouched by the swift bitch that should have struck him again as he regained his feet the second time, loosened his strong legs and started out, wolf fashion, to seek the safety of numbers and to add his strength to the strength of the little pack. The Master had made a terrible mistake of judgment. If, indeed, Zanoza's condition was such that she should not join the chase, she should have been left at home to take her daily exercise beside some peacefully trotting groom. Not that Krilatka and the Tearer could not run down any wolf that ever stole a sheep—not that—but because the Master did not realize how really great a team of hounds he had, nor what they would attempt. And so the leash that held the trembling Sweetheart almost disastrously wrecked the instinctive

team play of the three. Sure that she was to go out
with them, the two other dogs had set out to treble
the record of any coursing team in all Russia's wide
extent. But as the last wolf had escaped the Master's
spear, so now the second did likewise, and springing
unmolested to his feet, joined his companion and soon
left the Master far in the rear.

Krilatka the wise heard behind him, after a time,
the swish of snow. Suspicious, he left the pursuit
to the hot-headed Tersai, and dropped a little to the
rear, and took a glance back over his shoulder. Most
assuredly all was not well. No Zanoza in sight—no
Master—no kennelman, but scarcely half a hundred
leaps behind, two lolling tongues, two sets of hungry,
long, white teeth!

Here then was matter for thought; and leaping behind the headlong, eager, bloodthirsty Tersai, Krilatka,
wisest of all borzoi, menaced close behind by onrush-
ing, ignoble death, coolly planned his shrewd campaign

Tersai at first would not hear of it. Better to
turn at once and let a glorious battle decide the issue
None should ever say of him, Tersai, the Tearer-to
Pieces, that he had ever fled a wolf—or two—or even
three of that accursed breed! But at last the counsel
of the cool and wise prevailed, and the leaping wolf
was suddenly astonished to see his two pursuers jump
out ahead of him.

So now began the great White Falcon's masterpiece
of coursing, a hunt which will be the kennel talk of
Russia for a hundred years to come. Now started the

great circle. Side by side the two magnificent hounds
leaped out into the desolate steppe, away from the protection of horses and dogs and men, with a speed
which told the wolves at once that nothing could run
down that game but the endlessness of lupine endurance. And so, with the chase reversed, and the desire
for vengeance stronger than the urge of hunger in their
hearts, the three wild animals ceased their frenzied
bursts of fleeing speed and settled down to the easy
lope that had never failed, in the end, to wear down
every creature that their rapacious stomachs had ever
marked.

All through the morning the wolfhounds ran with
never a slackening of speed; and the flat steppe spread
away in front of them in endless whiteness. To travel
on anything but a straight line meant that the pursuers ran on the chord of the curve and so a shorter
distance. Besides, the wolves must never suspect that
they were running on anything but a straight line. So
for the latter reason, as well as from the necessity of
having the difference between arcs and chords as small
as possible, the circle had to be enormous; and the
White Falcon set his course and his great heart accord-
ingly.

Noon passed and the cold of evening came on, and
still the two grand borzoi stretched their long legs in
speed that was only equalled by the tenacity of their
pursuers.

The moon rose, and the Master's pony, hardly able
to walk from fatigue, came staggering in on the long

back trail that led to the forest edge where Mastov and Radyikk, beating their mittened hands against their sides, walked their ponies briskly up and down to keep them and the hounds from perishing of cold. The Master's head hung low. Moisture was frozen upon his beard at a point too high to have come from his breathing.

"We should have died before the sun came up," he said simply, and then started to lead the hunt toward home.

"Master," said Mastov Borloff, "see the Sweetheart."

The beautiful hound was spread out flat on her belly on the snow, the leash from her to the advancing pony stretched taut.

Baron Ladislaus Michaelovitch, of Astronov, one time had started to Siberia with a thousand offenders and with certain orders, the seal of which was not to be broken until he had reached the border town of Bolotova. At Bolotova he had broken the seal and, after reading the orders, had watched them shrivel to a black cinder with a very dreadful expression on his face.

But nevertheless, two months later, at Gorgievsk, he sent a message to St. Petersburg which said that he had managed to get the guard through safely so far without the loss of a man, but, he regretted to say, every one of the prisoners had succumbed to the rigours of the march. But now the voice of Ladislaus Michaelovitch came trembling pitifully out of his beard.

"There is no warmth in the moon, Mastov, my infant," he said, "and before the night should pass many dead *guanchi* and men would lie quiet in the snow."

So the cavalcade started again; but Zanoza's body merely dragged a pathway through the snow.

"Put her across the horse!" said the Master.

Mastov Borloff dismounted. For the first time in her life Zanoza lifted her lips as a human hand reached down to her.

"I will stay with her, Master," wept the stolid huntsman. "She is waiting for Krilatka. I will stay with her! He will come!"

"After these hours?" asked the Master, impatient of such sentimental nonsense. "Krilatka and the Tearer would have been back long ere this had it been God's will that they should come. You will die and the Sweetheart also; and I could not replace the Sweetheart—especially now, when the saving of her means that we may have another Krilatka. Come!"

"She knows," answered Mastov Borloff with dull Muscovite stubbornness. "I know, too, Master. I will stay. The White Falcon will bring them in—all three."

"Fool!" snapped Michaelovitch, loosening the knout at his saddle-bow. "Pick up the bitch!"

But Mastov Borloff merely stooped above the little *psovoi* and laid his protecting body over her. And then suddenly the heavy form of the huntsman was flung up to meet the descending whip. Six of the wire-wound thongs whipped round his hunting cap of fur, and found his flesh, and dragged a half dozen gashes across his cheek and forehead. But he never felt the cuts. He just stood motionless and stiff armed, in the awkward position into which the leaping bitch had heaved him, pointing a blunt mitten in the direction where the slender-yegged Zanoza was flitting away over the white steppe carpet. Far, far out in the indistinct silver of the moon five black specks had appeared.

"Hold fast all hounds!" roared suddenly the mighty voice of Baron Ladislaus Michaelovitch. "By Mary's sacred Ikon, those three shall do this glorious thing themselves!"

Mastov Borloff leaped with a single bound into his high saddle.

"Ai-e-e-e-e-e-agh!" shouted he; and he dashed off through the moonlight, while Radyikk Olnovsk sat his pony, and held in leash his trio of straining hounds, and plead with his patron saint to let the horse of that lucky fool Borloff step through the frozen roof of a marmot's burrow.

Far out on the plain the lips of Tersai had begun to lift up, every once in a while, in a snarl that told how the fangs that they uncovered would soon have to take up the work his legs could never finish. But low whimperings of encouragement came to him from the throat of Krilatka, who still leaped steadily on.

"Would not the Sweetheart be waiting for them at the end of this terrible circle?" he asked. "Was she not worthy to be in at the kill?" he reasoned with the terrible one. "Come now," he whined, "another half hour and the great ring will close."

But another half hour's top speed lay not in Tersai's long, flat-boned legs. Many more hours of wonderful speed was in them—true; but only highest speed, such as now they ran, would keep those hot teeth out of his stifles. And he, Tersai, the Tearer-to-Pieces, he would have his wounds in the front! And he was at the very point of wheeling to receive them there, when he heard the falcon-eyed one ask him what he made of the tiny, dim, moving speck approaching them, so far ahead! The Tearer strained his eyes and saw what the wolves had not yet seen, and a mighty overwhelming pride in his team mates blurred his sight, and the mighty joy in teamwork filled up his loyal, ferocious heart! Valiant little Sweetheart! Wise old Krilatka! He looked at the great White Falcon for advice. The grave lips of Krilatka wore a grin!

"Now!" roared he to Tersai.

And Tersai, who had been waiting through the long, long hours for that word, bunched up his legs, slid in his tracks and wheeled, and did what it was thought no other borzoi in all Russia would have dared.

And the foremost wolf, a monstrous, wicked fellow, in his surprise, trying frantically to check himself, bore down, sliding in the snow, upon a maw as gaping as his own, and into jaws more punishing and fangs more knifelike.

The other two wolves turned and fled. Krilatka spread the beautiful legs that were his peregrine pinions and swooped in swift pursuit; for now he plainly saw the form of the little Sweetheart skimming, toward the Tearer, over the snow. Suddenly then the wolf, lashing at the crazy Tersai, went down crashing; and as that borzoi devil bit into the overturned animal's jugular, Zanoza went flashing on past, to add her cunning to the cunning of her kennel mate.

The second wolf went down, sprawling and cutting out of sight in a white spray, before Zanoza came up to Krilatka, and instinctively she went on by. Somehow she knew that the wise white dog would never leave this wolf again until it was slain. Too long had been his labour and his peril, and too careful his planning, to risk the work of downing this great hell dog to the hot-headed Tersai. Right clearly his instinct told him that Tersai's berserk rage, so long restrained, and his pride, so long under the lash of ignominious pursuit, would hold him with his wolf till either he or the beast should be ripped to shreds.

Mastov Borloff, with the sting of the night in the raw cuts under his beard, rode like a devil to win the kill away from his own cruel master, and with his fresh pony outdistanced the baron's exhausted mount with ease. And the thick-haired little horse, proud of the fact that he, and not the Master's beast, made up the fourth indispensable unit of that Golden Trumpet wolf team, pounded to the aid of the three great hounds that were his friends at such a speed that his rider, sticking a skilful lance down into the white whirl that marked the spot where Krilatka had

knocked down his wolf for the fourth time, soon ended
that mighty combat.

Krilatka paused to vent no Tersai passion on the
form that writhed in death agony beside him, but,
leaping nimbly from beneath the pony's hoofs, sprang
away for the last mad stretch of that long chase. But
Mastov Borloff, galloping ahead, cursed vilely and
threw away his slender lance. The head of it had
snapped off between the ribs of Krilatka's wolf. Half
a verst ahead of him two racing forms merged into
one.

"Now Saint Methodius save the little bitch; and
curse to everlasting fire the Master who would not
listen to a kennel-man's advice to leave the little
Sweetheart home! For she has gone down with the
wolf!"

The huntsman grimly loosened the long dirk in the
belt about his blouse and kicked his heels wildly into
his pony's ribs. The little fellow answered gamely
with everything he had. And now the rider was close
enough to see the wolf rip at Zanoza as she lay
strangely motionless where she had gone down. The
Russian groaned. He rose to a stand in his high
saddle, as he galloped on, and pulled loose the dirk.
Then suddenly his groan turned to a yelp. Past him
shot a white form, with a speed that made it seem as
though the pony were standing still.

Spent was the White Falcon's flight when he struck
the wolf, and none knew it better than Krilatka. But
far from spent was the limitless endurance of the

wolf; for though to the borzoi is given great bursts of matchless speed that will last through minutes and hours, to the wolf is given a pace which, though less swift, lasts through hours and days. He runs for the first sun and moon on the meat of the last kill; and for the next day on the fat that helps his thick fur coat protect him from the cold; and for that night on the adipose that lies within his sinews; and for the next day on the very motor tissues themselves; and after that for as long a time as is necessary, till he pulls down the kill, on nothing but his will to run.

And Krilatka, knowing about this thing from the wisdom of his long-haired greyhound ancestors that may still be seen hunting with Cyrus on the ancient Persepolitan bas-reliefs at Shiraz, knew also that if ever the wolf got under way again the chase was done, for back in the snow, a verst away, the fool Tersai was still venting his selfish fury on a dead wolf.

And just beside him the little Sweetheart lay, strangely inert and listless, and his own mighty efforts of the day had drained dry the vessels of his speed. But, by the love of men, three wolves should be the bag of his team that day! For such an impossible record he had set out early in the bright morning. For such a record—because some fool had not unleashed the Sweetheart—he had had to lead the rebellious Tersai ahead of three gaunt wolves, on the rim of a great circle, all the long day and deep into the night. And for the completion of the record on which he had set his stalwart heart the royal borzoi, knowing his risk, did calmly and cool-headedly the thing that Tersai did with heart aflame!

He reached the wolf with the last vestige of his speed; but, as the beast went down from the blow of his shoulder, Krilatka made no effort to leap clear of the murderous teeth.

Instead he closed with him. And as the snow sprayed and tossed up in the moonlight, warm, dark splotches discoloured the icy spume.

That weird, chilling Cossack war yell, which argues better than any nice deductions of ethnology that the American Indian is no autochthon, wailed cruel-heartedly toward the moon. A lathered pony pounded past the frothing snow geyser, riderless. But a third figure now lashed confusedly about in the white froth. Down from out of the high, swaying saddle it had half toppled, half sprung, in a bone-cracking dive that had landed Mastov Borloff fair on the grey devil's back. And above the wicked snarling rose wickeder Slavish blasphemies; and above the white ferment rose a black arm and a dirk that flashed a moment in the moon before it drove down into the turmoil, and struck again, and thrice and four times, before the snow spray settled down and everything grew still.

So came to a glorious end the making of the Astro-novia record, which stands unbeaten to this day; but the greatest wonder of it is not known when, after much thick-shouldered shruggings of Muscovite ven-eration, it has been told how the Golden Trumpet team of three pulled down three of Satan's *volk* breed that night. The babble of heavy voices about the steaming samovar grows low and awed only when the tale comes to the very end, when they hear again in what condition the little Sweetheart took her part in that epic hunt.

For, at the end of the coursing, the Master stood not over the last of the great grey hell dogs; nor did the bleeding Mastov Borloff stop to gloat over his kill. And Krilatka, even, put off the licking of his wounds and joined the men where they stood; and with them he looked commiseratively down at the spot where Zanoza nosed three quiet little forms close in against the warmth of her thick-furred body.

"Two weeks before their time," sobbed the Master broken-heartedly.

But Mastov Borloff, who had the kennelman's instinct in such matters, suspected—hoped for, rather than detected—an infinitesimal stir among the huddled three.

"Master!" he called in a voice of awe. "See! The one marked black and tan and white, like her!"

The Master kneeled hastily in the snow beside Zanoza. And Krilatka rubbed his long, warm tongue across the Sweetheart's eyes. Then Mastov Borloff stooped and gathered her in his arms. It was the Master himself who helped his man to mount. It is said that the kennelman carried the seventy-five pounds of her so tenderly and so quietly on the long, slow night ride home that when they took her off of his stiff forearms to lay her on the rug before the fireplace,

and thawed from his hands the mittens that were stiff
with frozen blood, it was found that six of his fingers
were white to the second knuckle.

While they were rubbing his hands that were thrust
to the wrists in a bucket of snow, Zanoza lifted her
long head from the wide, warm pelt of the great Man-
churian bear and whined. And in her soft eyes
gleamed a light that only a woman could have seen,
when the Master reached his hand into the bosom of
his coat and, searching through the folds of blouse and
shirt and heavy undergarment, tenderly lifted out,
from against his heart, a little ball of down.

II

Last Friday night it rained. The day had been a cold
and grey and dismal one—such a day as has always
proved a bad one for the Bobl. And now, in the early
evening, when at last he had quieted and gone to sleep,
and Bobl's mother and I had gone to bed also, the
rain had come. I was awakened by the roar of it. It
deluged down upon the tin roof, just outside of our
window, in a perpendicular torrent. There was no
wind. No wind, it seemed to me, could have forced
a way through the solid wall of it, or found strength
enough to blow that downpour at any angle from the
vertical. Windless the rain fell, plumb out of heaven,
and beat upon the roof outside the window of our
room heavily, and heavier and heavier still, till I felt
that the housetop would surely give way under the
solid impact.

I quietly lay and listened with a sort of awe to the beat of it and to the pixie voices chattering in the splash of it. And surely and more surely heard the plaintive cry of Bobl, wailing among the other eerie voices. I told myself that this could not be; for always, no matter how bad the day that little Bobl spends, once sleep comes over him, his blessed, patient, tiny face composes itself to a slumber the soundness of which seems to vary directly with his geyserlike activities of the bygone day.

Those of us who know the proprietress well enough call the hotel at which small Bobl boards by various names. Sometimes it is known as the Quick Lunch, sometimes the Pension au Lait, sometimes, when we feel especially facetious, the Bawlsfor-Castoria. Known by whatever name, small Bobl was in imminent danger of being forced to move away from it last Friday; for the culinary department of this favourite caravansary of his was suddenly proving very inefficient. Desperate efforts had been made by the proprietress to give the guest a satisfactory service. In at the supply door had come unlimited quantities of the raw materials of the dish that seemed to be the small itinerant's favourite. Cocoa and chocolate by the hundredweight, malted milk in endless jars, oranges by the crate, porter in cases (making entrance surreptitiously for the first time in at the supply door of a strictly temperance house), and lastly an unbelievably vile concoction of the most nauseating fats collectible; all of these Bobl's hostess downed heroically, with the great fear of growing fat gnawing at her heart, and with such facial contortions at the last of them as proved against my absolutest convictions that her countenance under some circumstances could form a really unattractive bit of scenery. But these various supplies, for all the sustenance they furnished the one guest at the hostelry in question, might just as well have been poured into the gutter. The kitchen of that inn failed utterly to transform its raw goods into the staple that it so proudly flaunted on its menu under the appetizing name of Boblgrub.

And so through that gloomy, long last Friday, the fastidious guest had roared his protest at the service, until at last, despairing at the frantic failures of his hostess to provide the single item that was printed so alluringly on the bill of fare, he refused any longer to appear at the table at meal times; but attempted, as many another man had done before him, to drown his sorrows in the bottle. Dozens he emptied greedily, bottoms up, only to bring their contents forth into the light of the world again with a regularity, dependability, and altitude of jet which would have put Old Faithful to shame.

But at last the little guest had hushed his clamours in sleep. And I had witnessed that wonderful sight which is to be seen when such proprietresses as Steve tuck in their weary, tiny, hungry guests; and I had seen, with a peculiar fulness at the throat the splashing drops that never fail to fall upon pink blankets that are snuggled about such wee unsatisfied boarders as have stilled their protests in exhausted, empty-bellied sleep.

So I felt sure, as I listened to the thundering rain and the ghostly voices wailing in it, that my imagination was playing me tricks, and that my ears had simply not ceased to register the vibrations that had cried into them all day. I lay still, trying to dissuade myself that any small voice lamented in the downfall, when my wife's weary voice said:

"Isn't that Bobl crying?"

She, too, then, had heard this ghost cry in the splash of the rain.

"Go to sleep, Steve," I answered boldly. "Don't let your imagination be playing you tricks."

The room itself was absolutely quiet. Outside the drops must have been falling close enough together to gather in great balls, so fierce was the pounding on the adjacent roof. And steadily persistent in it came the faint cry. Small was the Bobl, but mighty were his lungs. Never, since the very minute of his arrival in our midst, had his voice been accused of faintness. "Therefore," said I to myself, "when he speaks there will be no doubt about it. He will make himself heard plainly enough above the hammering of the rain." But, just the same, the small, mysterious voice kept sounding. And at the appeal of it, a sense of ugly, spectral menace came upon me. I heard the uneasy squeak of springs beside me.

"Be still," I said. "I'll go and see."

My feet found the slippers. Groping through the

bathroom door I became positive that the sound of crying from the grey room, where the Bobl slept, was purely a matter of imagination. I opened the door.

A snarl that acted like an astringent on my spine came out of the dark corner where the cradle was. Quickly I snapped on the light. The gathered muscles of the crouching animal went lax. A busy tail waved. My blood started to run again. Little Bobl's closed eyelids contracted a trifle in the light; but the blessed face that showed above the close-tucked blanket stayed serene in sleep. It had been all imagination then. "Zanoza, Sweetheart," I whispered, "how did you get in here?"

Then back of me I heard the silky slip of naked feet. I wonder how great a chain would have to be lashed round her bed to keep Steve in it if she thought she heard that little Bobl cry!

"I left the door from the balcony open on purpose," she confessed. She put down her hand caressingly on the long, sharp muzzle of this truly lucky dog.

"It's all tommyrot," she pouted up to me, "this talk of jealousy." Then, "Isn't it, Zanoza?" she whispered to the bitch. "You love the baby, don't you, Sweetheart?"

After that snarl that had greeted me from the dark my doubts were also cleared.

"Wait here a minute, Steve," I said to Bobl's mother.

I went out on the back balcony and got the mat of cedar shavings out of the long box, and brought it back into the grey room and laid it down beside the baby's cradle.

"I am all unstrung today," said Steve. "Such weird, uncanny fears for the boy's safety have been stealing over me tonight as I lay listening to the voices in that terrible rain! But they go away when I see the Sweetheart curled up by his bed."

And I myself, as I snapped off the light again, felt a great, sweet sense of security in my heart, because of the mental picture that I took with me out of the grey room, of that long, black-and-tan-and-white, faithful lady curling herself to sleep beside the little fellow, whom I love even more than I love her. Those who are so inclined may sniff at this last comparison of affections. But there are certain things that those who are not dog lovers do not know. I, for instance, know that some cheerful morning, after a sleep very much longer than the one baby and his protector were sharing when we left them last Friday night, the long, graceful hound will come bounding, at Bobl's side, up the sands of some Elysian beach to meet me.

The mother slept. The rain continued. And the wan cry still sounded tenaciously in the roaring of it; but sure now that it lived in my mind alone, I, too, composed myself to sleep. Then, just as I was dozing off, the shrill clatter of our door-phone bell sounded above the rain. I slipped out of bed carefully; but my precaution was unnecessary. There was only one sound that would break that weary slumber. I pressed the switch that lighted the hall and, as I stepped into it, Zanoza passed me, gliding noiselessly, bristling a bit, toward the head of the steps, where she paused and stood growling ominously down to the entrance door of our apartment, which is on the floor below.

I stood a moment with the receiver in my hand and gazed at her, in the never-ending wonder of how utterly beautiful she was. For consummate loveliness—the borzoi! At times, looking at her, I had found myself wishing that, instead of the equivalent for swiftness, the Russian word for beauty were the name of the wolfhound breed. But I shall never have that wish again after last Friday night. Not even though I am surer now than ever that there is no created thing, quick or inanimate, so perfectly beautiful—except woman. From the tip of Zanoza's underswung tail to the point of her exquisite muzzle, the outlines of her were nothing else than the continuous soft melting of a series of Hogarth's ill-fated, graceful, serpentine S-lines of absolute beauty, one into the other.

That tiny black-and-tan-and-white bundle of fur which had come to our apartment about two years ago had turned out to be an appropriate and clever joke of my friend Whitely—practical in more ways than one. For what could have been more disconcerting to us humble flat dwellers than to see this ball of down develop into a lanky, floppy, ranging pup who treasured in her long, good-natured skull the ineradicable hope that some day she could make the trip from one end of our apartment to the other without marking her trail with a litter of upset furnishings?

Being as totally unaware, at that time, of what her breed might be as though she were a moon puppy, her adolescent stage was one long period of disgrace to us—a condition that Whitely, doubtless, had foreseen and was enjoying mentally to the utmost. If ever an animal looked as though its ancestry were a matter best left to the kindly obscurity of the untraced past, it was this long-legged, bony misfit. And then, all of a sudden, we ceased to hide her when our guests arrived. We trained her, instead, always to stand at the head of the steps to greet them; for, almost overnight, we had a Russian wolfhound in the family.

As to her quiet dignity and her complacent aristocracy of bearing, here the thoroughness of Whitely's joke reached its climax. Imagine, if you will, this Diana of the broad Russian steppes housed in our plebeian five rooms, kitchen, pantry, living hall and bath! But though we felt that she was out of her class with us, she settled down quietly and, without the slightest show of condescension, worked her sweet way into our city-dwelling hearts, so deeply and contentedly that none would have ever thought that she dreamed—before the abominable gas logs of our imitation of a real fireplace—ancestral dreams of a fierce chase, in which her grandsire and her grandam had won eternal fame, and her own mother had been prematurely whelped in a pool of wolf's blood.

But now as I answered the door-phone, Zanoza

stood at the head of our stairs and snarled at the entrance door an intuitive snarl that shed some light upon the nature of her fireside dreams.

"Doctor Lucas?" I questioned into the transmitter.

"No, no, Lupus," laughed the peculiar voice from downstairs. "L-u-p-u-s," And although I didn't realize why at the time, the name had something in it that made the goose pimples rise on my skin.

"I have a letter of introduction from our mutual friend, Clarence Whitely, of Philadelphia," continued the voice.

"Oh," I shouted down the wire to him, all my doubts dispelled, "in that case you can't get up our steps fast enough."

I pulled the rope of my bathrobe tighter at my waist and waited for him with Zanoza, at the head of the stairs.

He wore a great fur coat of tannish gray—a skin I did not know. I thought at first it was the rain on this that brought a strong, peculiar, familiar, disagreeable odour into the hall. But upon sighting the hound beside me, Doctor Lupus halted suddenly. I thought he paled a little. Then, folding the coat, fur inside, he laid it on the floor of the lower hall, just outside the door.

"It is too wet," were the first words he said, in answer to the protest that my lips must have formed. "I will not drip your rugs with it," and, closing the door, he came up the stairs to meet me, smiling most engagingly. But the strong odour still persisted. I reached down my left hand, while I was shaking his, and buried my fingers in Zanoza's beautiful coat, thinking perhaps she had got wet on the back balcony; but her hair was warm and dry. I felt uncomfortable —strangely.

The doctor was as handsome a man as ever I have met, and as affable a gentleman. And I had not talked with him ten words, there at the head of the stairs, before I was at ease with him, although the stuffy odour still persisted. He knew Whitely very well. In the spontaneity of the greeting that I could not but extend to a friend of one of my best friends, I stood there at the top of the steps, pleasantly chatting, several minutes before I excused my dress and the absence of Mrs. Church and waved him to the easy-chair that opened its arms only to my most favoured guests.

I paused, while he went ahead, to switch on the light that would brighten the far end of the corridor. The doctor was walking through the dimly lighted hall with the Sweetheart at his side. All the strange uneasiness that she had shared with me seemed to have passed at the sound of his voice, at the touch of his hand and at the sight of him. I forgot at the time that the borzoi is a sight hound. Besides, the familiar, somewhat disagreeable odour had entirely vanished.

The button under my finger snapped and the hall flooded with light, just as the doctor was passing the hall rack. He paused before the mirror and put his hand up to his tie. With a snarl that was twenty times as vicious as the one that had greeted my entrance to the grey room a little while before my hound crashed wildly into the glass.

"Zanoza!" I called in a sharp, low voice. "Fool dog! Do you want to wake the lady?"

She stood with her front paws on the seat that ran beneath the mirror, growling wickedly at her reflection in the glass.

"Fool doggy," I said to her again, and stroked her long face. "Since when have you started to take exceptions to your own reflection?"

"The sudden light did seem to make her image leap right out at her," explained the doctor, from his seat in my guest chair at the far end of the hall. He was just finishing the removal of his second glove. He had not started to unbutton the first when he left the head of the stairs. In the confusion of the dog's peculiar behaviour, I had not noticed the doctor, but he must have moved from that mirror as though the devil were after him to have reached the chair so quickly.

"There is a baby in your house then?" said he, flashing his beautiful but somewhat sharp, white teeth in genial interest. "Whitely never told me this bit of news."

"I never told Whitely about it," I explained. "He promised to come visit me next month, and I am hoping to surprise him. You must not speak of the arrival when you see him again."

Zanoza, still grumbling to herself, slipped past me, stiff-legged and bristling, and looked round the corner of the hall desk behind which the doctor now sat. Then her tail switched kindly reassurance, and she hung her head a trifle shamefacedly, I thought. I knew just how she felt. Just as we were talking about the baby I, too, imagined that I had smelled the thick, familiar odour strongly again.

I assured the doctor that I was only too glad to remain awake for the evening and to relieve the day's strain by a conversation that would include news from Whitely.

"He said," laughed Doctor Lupus, "that I should be his proxy in the matter of smelting a little brass for you before I left."

And at this evidence of his intimacy with Whitely a normal state of mind returned to me. There are two lines of activity in which my old friend and roommate excels. One is an alchemy by which he transmutes worn-out alarm-clock works and similar base rubbish into shining coinage of the realm, *via* his little tin-horn smelting furnaces. The other is the constant perpetration on his friends of the subtlest and kindliest of practical jokes—trickeries that always have the shrewdest turn to them—the very finest appropriateness; as witness his sending me a wolfhound puppy as a cure, I afterwards learned, for what he is pleased to term the most serious of my various mental ailments.

Ultra-practical Whitely claims that no man who

pretends to build blast furnaces for a living, as I do,
has any right to waste his evenings poring over musty
old volumes of wolf myths. He has no right to bore
his friends with the weird tales which the ignorant
peasantry, in that hotbed of superstition ringed by
the semicircle of the Carpathian Alps, tell and retell
each other, in order to make as miserable as possible
their bitter winter nights.

I, on my part, though never voicing any objection
to that black art of Whitely's, to which the doctor
had made reference, so long as he confines it to his
plant along the Delaware, have often taken exception
to his practice of melting overtime his confounded
copper and zinc and tin, in my library, in the rare
evenings when we get together. And so, at the mention of the smelting of brass, at once an ease in the
doctor's presence which I had not felt before descended
on me.

"May I?" he said, after we had been chatting
pleasantly a while; and he brought forth a most peculiar pipe from out of one of his pockets. It was
black, well caked and short-stemmed; the bowl of it
a wonderfully wrought, hideously grinning skull; the
eye sockets and the nose and mouth openings of some
transparent substance, so that, when he smoked, the
fire of his tobacco first made the eyes gleam evilly,
later the nose, and lastly lit up the teeth ingeniously
in the most hellish sort of a grin.

He extended to me a very black cigar. I told him
that I was a charter member of the Purity League and

did not use the weed; whereupon he seemed more disappointed than was natural, but started to stuff into that grisly pipe of his an odd, tannish, grey-coloured tobacco, the like of which I had never seen before, and the like of which, thank heaven, I had never smelled before. As he lay back smiling and gossiping in my chair and began to partake of the comfort of that short-stemmed death's head, a reek so foul ascended from it that I could hardly forbear hoisting the window beside me.

Zanoza sniffed; then, with the delicacy of perfect breeding, she indicated her disapproval of the use of nicotine in the presence of a lady by quietly rising and excusing herself, with the customary thrust of her long nose under my elbow. She put out a paw and opened the bathroom door. As she went sedately through it toward the door that opened into Bobl's room, I called to her:

"Take good care of that little girl of yours, Sweetheart!"

"How's this?" exclaimed Doctor Lupus quickly, with a deprecating smile.

"She's not a bit jealous," I told him. "I might be the least bit dubious about a dog, but I trust her absolutely. Some day," I laughed, but was serious, "she will have children of her own."

The doctor smiled indulgently.

"It's not a matter of violence, but of hygiene. I myself thoroughly agree with the man who said that every child has a perfect right to be raised with a dog. But not too intimately—especially in infancy. How many other children's faces does your hound lick in friendliness for them? We are so very doubtful, our profession, as to just how certain germs are carried."

I got up at once and went through the bathroom. Again the ugly snarl startled me, as I opened the other door; and again I hastened to snap on the light and saw a wickedness, of which I had not thought Zanoza capable, fade from her face as her uplifted lips let down. Once again the indefinable sense of fear chilled me, and once again the warmth of the long hound's protecting presence at the cradle chased away the foolish presentiment. The room was cold; as usual Bobl's window was wide open. The rain had changed to snow. I tiptoed over to the cradle, to see if the young scout had pawed the covers away from his throat. Somehow sensing my presence, the tiny face puckered in its sleep; but a contented little noise, half squeak, half grunt, told me that all was well. I touched the blanket where it was tucked under his chin, not because it did any good, but because I couldn't help it.

"Come, Sweetheart," I said, banishing the strange fear that still cried for the reassurance of her presence with the boy.

Only the very tip of the silk-furred tail stirred.

"Come, girlie," I insisted; "the doctor says that you might lick the young fullback's face."

But she refused to be persuaded. I think that I

wanted to let her stay as much as she desired it. Eerie premonitions would not down in my mind—nor in hers. But I put aside the witless forebodings.

"Now! Now!" I said to her firmly. These are the harshest words I ever have to use to her. So she rose up very reluctantly, and before following after me, laid her long muzzle on top of the pink blanket that inclosed half the world. I wish I had a picture that would show the look that shone in her mild eyes as she stood in all her stately dignity and beauty beside that little wooden bed. It broke my heart to make her come away.

When I returned from the back balcony I noticed immediately that the doctor was no longer in the hall. The light was burning in the bathroom and I could hear the sound of running water through the open door. That heavy odour, which was the natural perfume of a wet dog, but triple extracted, the cause of an unconquerable fear in my heart, now rose strongly even above the disguising reek of the doctor's pipe. I shivered a bit.

Just then the knocker on my door clicked softly. I started as though the noise had been a pistol shot I pressed the button that released the latch at the foot of the stairs. It was a messenger boy, snow powdered on the shoulders.

The door closed quietly. The clatter of the boy's feet on the stairs came to me less and less clearly Three floors below I heard the entrance door slam faintly shut, with that peculiar muffled quality o

sound that exists when the air is full of snow. The
spigot in the bathroom closed off with a chug. The
house was very quiet. I heard a rattle at the door
that led from the pantry out onto the balcony. A
wind had commenced to stir outside, or did another
thing disturb the door? Did I hear a wistful whining
at it, as though Zanoza knew how badly she was
needed inside at that moment? And still I stood like
a fool and stared at that night letter.

It was signed Whitely. It said:

Church: Sending Lupus to you to find out whether
I am nutty or suffering from the same disease I sent
you cure for a year or two ago; also because I think you
know more about lycanthropy than any living man, and
because you have her at the house. Get a mirror back of
him and, if you see what I saw, turn her loose on him!

With my whole body tingling in a horrid chill I
tiptoed swiftly to the other door that gave entrance
from the hall into the grey room. I picked up the
long paper knife as I went past the hall desk. The
cursed latch squeaked as I turned the knob. I could
have sworn that I saw a waving tip of bushy grey disappear into the lighted oblong of the bathroom door
as I leaped into the room. The unmistakable smell
of a wet, unclean dog smote on my nostrils. I sprang
to the cradle, my blood icy with fear. Then Doctor
Lupus stepped very quietly from the bathroom into
my presence, a partly emptied glass of water in his
hand. He took a swallow from the tumbler and

smiled a smile that made me feel like an imbecile. I slipped the long knife up my bathrobe sleeve, thanking heaven for the gloom of the room that had prevented his catching a glimpse of it. A day of worry over the firstborn surely makes an idiot of a man.

"I took the liberty of drawing a drink while you were arguing matters over with the dog," he whispered, grinning pleasantly, "and as I thought I heard you stirring in the men's ward here, I wondered if I might be allowed to look upon the new construction engineer."

With proper pride, diluted this time by a saving humiliation at the wildness of my fancies, I motioned him over to the cradle. He looked down somewhat eagerly at the tender little face. His gleaming teeth flashed cordially in the dusk across the sleeping boy to me.

"Congratulations," he whispered. "Some son! I am very fond of babies."

And at his last words I became suddenly aware of the night letter crinkling in my bathrobe pocket and of the long-bladed paper knife inside my bathrobe sleeve.

Two low windows open from my dining room out onto the back balcony, which is on the sunset end of our apartment. The buffet stands along the south wall of the room. I had pulled out the chair which sits with its back to the buffet, and the doctor, after glancing casually about the room, and especially back of him, had seated himself in it. I tilted the coffee urn.

"Sugar?"

He nodded.

I rose and walked round the table to the sideboard and procured the silver bowl. The doctor sat smiling contentedly and blowing rings of his vile tobacco smoke up into the cluster of frosted light globes. I reached back and quietly dropped the cover off of the buffet mirror as I leaned over the doctor's shoulder.

"One or two?" I asked, with the tongs poised. "You are sure you can't stay over with us tonight?" I inquired; and I glanced back over my shoulder.

What I saw in the mirror turned my soul sick.

Like a great hulking fool I had, at first opportunity, slipped the knife out of my sleeve, and it now lay on the mantel above the fireplace, back of my chair, on the other side of the table. I dropped the two lumps into the devil's cup without splashing a drop.

I reached my seat in absolute calmness, though my head buzzed from the volumes of rank vapour that rolled from that skullheaded pipe. I poured myself some coffee. Then I reached back of me; but I didn't turn my head to do it.

"Did you ever see a more beautiful paper knife?" I asked him, extending it, handle first, across the table. It was a genuine barong; the blade as thin as paper, the handle of the very creamiest ivory, wonderfully carved and inlaid. A classmate of mine, who had helped erect the mills and furnaces at Tatta, had sent it to me.

My manner must have totally disarmed him. He

examined the beautiful instrument admiringly, and I looked into the mirror meanwhile. The trembling of my outstretched hand came more from hate than from the sickening fear that at first had palsied me.

"It is wonderfully beautiful," he said at length. "May I ask where you got it?" And he took hold of the wide, supple blade by its needle point and handed it back to me. I am sure that my face was altogether composed; but my will must have been so occupied with facial control that I forgot entirely how expressive the human hands may be. My fingers must have wrapped themselves about that graceful handle with an eagerness that even its original Moro owner could never have matched.

Tobacco? It was the very smoke of hell that he puffed suddenly fair in my face as we leaned over the table toward each other. I swayed dizzily in my chair. The doctor rose and lifted his lips in a smile. He bowed gracefully. But back of him, in the mirror, I saw with dimming eyes the beast first drop his front paws to the floor. Then his hind quarters slouched down gracefully; and at last, when I shifted my glazing eyes from the image to the object, I saw the doctor's form stoop and disappear below the edge of the table.

My voice would not come up. The reek of that pipe pulled down like leaden weights upon my eyelids. But my dimming ears caught the sound of a click against the window that gave out upon the balcony. I looked. A gleam of fangs shone out of the dark beyond the panes. And a snarl—snarl that I knew and loved—came to my dulling senses and stimulated them to one great effort.

"Zanoza!" I managed to shriek out hoarsely. But that sweet sight hound needed no call from me. Across three thousand miles of ocean and three thousand miles of land and down across three thousand years another call had come to her. No longer did her untrustworthy nose tell her indefinitely the truth about my guest. Her keen sight-questing eyes had seen below the level of my table a transformation that no eyes of earth had ever seen before.

Straight through the stout, splintering frame and jingling glass she came, this picturesque daughter of Zanoza Second, of Astronov, who was the daughter of the first Zanoza, eyes wild with wildness of the chase, and in a second was tearing with frantic needle fangs at the panels of the closed door that led out into the hall. A breath of the sweet, cold air blew through the shattered window and swept away the stench of Gehenna out of my nostrils. I leaped upon my feet. I weighed two hundred. I never stopped to unlatch the door into my hall.

Halfway down the stairs I heard the purring of a huge motor. Ah, Ephraim Johnson, you coloured handy man at the garage, if only you are drunk once more this night! For you have promised to come for the little car that I left standing in front of the apartments.

Three-quarters way downstairs my eyes went blind

at the sight of a small pink blanket lying pitifully crumpled on the steps. My eyes went blind a second; but my fingers simply loved the ivory handle of that sweet barong.

I never thanked John Barleycorn for anything before; but when I saw my little car, rain washed, snow sprinkled, still standing at the curb, I could have gone down on my knees in gratitude for his service in laying Mr. Johnson low again; for had not that sooty gentleman succumbed once more to some one of John's many blandishments my car had been standing inaccessible in the garage, two blocks away.

The powerful little engine flung my roadster down into the public square in the centre of the sleeping town. The lone policeman there cast a squat shadow on the snow under the clicking arc as he stood and blinked his astonishment at me. With a traffic-man's instinct he extended his hand. The shadow of his arm leaped out from the grotesque silhouette of his body and laid a shadowy barrier across my path. I only whisked the little car over the black bar and round into the street that led to the river. My judgment had been right.

Straight away the long bridge reached, silent and lonely; a ribbon of white, under its strings of incandescents, stretched tight across the river to the twinkling cluster of lights on the other side. Out beyond these lights lay a few miles of suburbs, then a long stretch of farm lands, then the woods. And the long car rolling ahead of me, halfway across the river, leaped and leaped in its effort to reach the timber. So started that wild exotic coursing last Friday night.

The bridge was far behind us, and the suburb also, when the moon came out. On each side of the road, behind snake fences, black farmhouses flew rearward out of sight. And in my staid, urban heart surged for the first time the thrill of mankind's most ancient sport, the chase. Ahead of me the quarry, and the lust for killing in my blood; and under me, not now the sway and thunder of saddle and hoofs, but instead the pulse and throb and leap of the machine. The gears whined eagerly. I felt the sinews of the car right in my very hands. My fingers sensed the pound and blow of every piston stroke, as they hammered their power into the wheels spinning beneath me; and the steady croon and whir of the whole machine sang music. And my left hand gripped, with wide curving fingers, its double hold upon the steering wheel and that lovely ivory handle.

But if the horrid fears that crowded my heart had been forced out by the raptures of the hunt, what unalloyed savage joy must have swelled to bursting in the deep chest of that long beast that ate up the road, halfway between that dreadful car and mine. The song of the *guanchi* rang in her racial memory, and Cossack shouts; and the scent of things no longer puzzled her nose. She had seen! And this flying house into which had stepped her quarry should no more get out of her sight! And she laid her long, beautiful body down close to the snow, and she ran.

No living creature ever ran as she. I saw that the car was not losing her. I saw that my own little roadster was not gaining on her; and I looked at the meter, but could not believe what was recorded there, for I tell you that I was not gaining on her!

Speed, the defence of the timid, was her attack! Speed, sheer speed, her death weapon! The long, sharp fangs that lined her punishing jaws were shield and coif to her—mere speed, unmatchable and terrible, her sword. So some wonderful artificer had made her. The very bones of her legs, which had to be mighty, made up the necessary section by being wide and flat, the long diameter of them running in the back and front direction, so as to offer little wind resistance. Her front was narrow. The mighty chest wherein lay lungs of greatest oxygenating power, provided ample room by reason of great vertical depth, there being almost no spring of ribs to spread her chest against the wind. Here she surpassed even her relative, the greyhound, in speed design. And her nose was long and pointed and went into the wind like an arrow, the soft ears folded back so tightly that the tips of them actually lapped. No stomach—the line from chest to loins curved up in marvellous beauty so close to the spine that it seemed to threaten the severance of the hind quarters altogether.

No stomach—just lungs and a mighty heart on four legs—and a brain. And that certain gauntness that challenges but never can discount the beauty of the greyhound here was covered up and hidden under a

Russian winter garment of fur, silky and curly and thick and long. Made for unspeakable loveliness and terrific speed was she and, as she opened and shut her long limbs back of that horrid car, delicate beauty flowed from her like melody, and the wonder grew as to how the bold heart to hunt the craftiest and fiercest of her family happened to throb inside a form whose every aspect gave out, in such measure as to overwhelm all other impressions, the appearance of surpassing elegance.

As I drove in that mad race the wonder of the fingent hands of man came over me, and of how the whole world is plastic under his touch. Out of the very wolf breed that he had abhorred he had taken specimens and had moulded and shaped them in his fingers, like some fictile matter, till he had evolved a tractable, gentle new kind of wolf that overmatched the first in speed and strength and courage and—greatest wonder —hated its own ancestors with a hatred that rooted down into the remotest fibres of its being.

But suddenly I was aroused from my thoughts by the far-off bang of an exploding tire. My eyes drew away from the fascination of the beautiful beast I had been watching, and my heart filled, half and half, with joy and apprehension. A half mile ahead I could see distinctly where the snow blew up in a little cloud from the sudden blast of the fiendish doctor's blowout; but only a scant half mile farther on, there loomed black under the moon that long low stretch of wooded hill that was the monster's goal.

A swift form dropped out of the big car and started off across the white level fields on a bee line toward the hills. So now it was Zanoza's great task to make up the quarter mile between her and her ghastly quarry in a short half mile of running. A stern chase is a long chase. Yet this one did not dare be long. So this Zanoza Third, who had lived her life in the confines of a city apartment, called back into the past for the hawk eye of the great White Falcon. And the keen vision of her grandsire came to her, so that she never lost sight of her quarry. No werewolf cunning was quite subtle enough to hide from her a glimpse of his flight, as she topped the rises back of him.

She demanded of her blood the speed of Krilatka also, and Krilatka's mighty lungs within her burned clean the waste of her terrible efforts. And fast as the great heart pumped in the turbid blood, it sent it out again instanter to the hungry straining sinews, sparkling and clear and red. Her forelegs reached out far ahead of her and dragged back the frozen ground to where her back feet could get hold of it; and then the great gaskin sinews, working through cunning powerful leverages of stifle and hock, kicked back that spot of earth that her rear paws held, full fifteen feet behind her. One moment she was a furry huddle of concentrated muscles, the next she was a long, outstretched, reaching symphony of borzoi curves, the silk fur from her brisket brushing the snow. And so, with the peregrine eye and flight and courage of

the dead and gone but still beloved Krilatka aiding
her, she bundled close and opened wide her powerful
long legs in a speed so frictionless, smooth and amaz-
ing that before the hell dog had reached the dark,
where the shadows of trees stretched out opposite the
lowhung moon, he felt on his rump the heat of Zanoza's
breath. Well may the fear of God shrivel your grisly
heart now, Doctor Lupus; for here at your wolfish
side bounds Zanoza Third, daughter of Zanoza Second
of Astronov, who was whelped prematurely, in a very
welter of lupine blood, at the end of the wonder hunt
of Russia.

I saw the little Sweetheart smash her high shoulder
down on top of his as she struck with the weapon of
her speed. I saw the cleverness of the first Zanoza
leap in her body, as she cleared the slashing fangs
that whirled at her and slipped behind the shield of
her own sharp teeth. And she knocked him down
again, gnashing desperately as he regained his feet.
I think, but for the training of her ancestors, this
elegant lady, reared in the enervating environment of
the fourth floor of a downtown apartment, would have
surely closed for the death with this hellish wolf.
But something told her that she must hold him for
the huntsman's lance; and so, for the third time, the
brave little *psovoi* launched her seventy-five pounds
of deadly speed toward the tan-furred shoulder—and
she struck Doctor Lupus fairly at the waist and
spilled him headlong!

He struggled up to hands and knees. I could hear

him calling to her first in a stern, then in a terror-stricken voice. For this daughter of the ancient sight-hunting breed had seen; and no touch, nor voice, nor scent could overweigh the testimony of what her eyes had watched take place below the level of my dining-room table. And before he could even get his hands out of the snow, she struck him down again.

One long, heavy timber took me fairly across the eyes as my doughty little roadster went through her fourth rail fence; but I clung to the wheel and the sweet barong and shook the blood out of my eyes as we rocked and lurched across the frozen furrows of that last rough field. She had just knocked him down the last time when the car went by them and broke itself to bits against the first trees of the wood that the gruesome creature had so nearly reached.

My leap was true. Going through the air at over thirty miles an hour, the cushion of his body was all that saved me from sudden death. My eyes were blind with blood from the blow of the flying rail, but I could feel quite horribly and plainly his throat beneath my fingers, and I could hear the voice of Doctor Lupus crying to me. I brushed my eyes clear of blood with my forearm as I lifted my left hand high. His face was white as death; his voice pitiful with terror. The blood from my forehead shut out the ghastly fear that shone in his fine eyes, and the baleful hate that glared from the eyes of her who lay close beside me, panting her exhaustion, her lips

updrawn, her muzzle hungrily close up against the
doctor's soft white throat.

I wrapped the fingers of my left hand greedily
about that ivory handle, and I drove the paper-thin
blade blindly down. I thought I felt the smooth skin
under my fingers become covered with a thick coat
of hair. I know that as I wildly drove my left arm
down and drove and drove again the shrieking of his
voice changed into long-drawn, agonizing ululations.

I didn't look to see what lay beneath me when silence
came at last, but rushed back over the fields to the
road and the terrible doctor's car, to find out what
it contained. With a heart to which a heart of mer-
cury would have been feather-light I called the Sweetheart to me and asked her what to do. She sniffed
at the little puppy that lay on the front cushion beside the driver's seat, and bristled and snarled and
pulled against her collar. I had known before she
confirmed my hideous fears what thing followed from
a werewolf's bite that was not fatal; but I held fast
to Zanoza's collar just the same.

I went back, leading Zanoza, and recovered an undamaged tire from the wreck of my car. Poor little
helpless puppy! Hopes and plans and motherings
and fatherings and depths of love that could never be
sounded mocked at me ghastlily from that downy
form. If only I had let Whitely know that a baby
had arrived at our house! Then the gruesome hope
and certainty came to my heart, as I watched the little
wolfling, that it would not always be like this. And

my wife was at home asleep, after her hard day with her baby. How could I go back to her empty-handed? How wake her in the morning? Like a coward I laid down the knife I held ready in my hand.

I let loose my hold on Zanoza's collar and stepped over into the driver's seat. The engine started to turn over. Then in the low rumble of it I heard that familiar snarl again—a whimper—good God, the little cry that had wailed to me in the roar of the rain! And as the car started I caught a glance of Zanoza worrying at something along the margin of the road. I knew that the cruel thing she did was right; the seat at my side was empty; but I bowed my head upon the wheel and drove home blindly through the night.

How we got back to town I do not know. I sneaked like a murderer up the stairs. Dawn had come; and with it the rain again. I thanked God for that. In the clatter of it I slunk unheard to bed. My head had hardly touched the pillow before I heard again the mockery of that little cry in the splashing of the downpour—more plainly now than ever.

She awoke.

"Bobl!" she said; and her voice was happy. "He wants the first of his three breakfasts."

Nausea ate at my heart. But she would sleep this last night through—of that I was determined!

"It is the rain," I told her, "just as before. You need the rest so badly, Stevie. Go to sleep."

"It is the boy," she said. The illusion of his voice was absolutely perfect in the rain. She put her hand up to her bosom and winced with pain; and I knew then why the contentment sounded in her voice. "I believe," and her voice was hungry with hope, "that Bobl won't have to hunt another boarding house after all. Won't you get him for me?"

At least I could lie to her. I took my bathrobe off of one of the four posts and went with staggering steps through the bathroom and opened Bobl's door. A snarl! The blood stopped in my veins. A friendly thump! It flowed again as my sick heart blessed her and all of her noble race, from Chihuahua to Saint Bernard. Loyal even to the empty crib! A little wail! I leaned up against the door jamb and my grief-withered heart filled out and swelled to the bursting point.

The glisten of a small, red head against a skin compared to which the creamy ivory of the handle of my Malay paper knife is sooty—who can describe it? And who, including you and Whitely, if he reads this, has any right to any such description?

I knotted the cord of my bathrobe.

"Aren't you coming back to bed? It's only four o'clock!" asked an amazed, soft voice.

"Not me!" I said good-bye to her, in a manner approved by all parties concerned, and left the Bobl sitting up to the breakfast table like a man—and his mother wondering.

I twisted the light button and opened up the steam valve in the library. Morpheus, patron of the most mysterious of the mental activities of men, is a persuasive, drowsy, procrastinating scalawag. Too often had he falsely convinced my over-receptive mind that adventures so extremely vivid in the night would all come back to me clearly for the writing in the morning!

White Monarch and the Gas-House Pup

McDonald's Grip and Mr. Slugs O'Boyle had just rounded the northeast corner of Madison Avenue and Twenty-sixth Street when the White Monarch's limousine drew up to the curb; and, simultaneously with the opening of the door of the car, the leash in Mr. O'Boyle's huge fist snapped rigid. And the White Monarch of Glenmere, stepping lazily down from his car, suddenly turned solid in his tracks.

Miss Audrey deHavin screamed and caught her skirts up about her so hastily and high that approximately ten dollars' worth of golden silk hosiery flashed into the view of an appreciative metropolis.

Mr. Forsythe Wentworth deHavin, who was handing her out of the Monarch's car, called out a command in a voice of mezzo-tenor sternness.

"I say, fellow," he said loftily, "hold more tightly to your leash there! You'll have your beastly cur upon the Monarch in a moment."

Mr. A. Beckwith deHavin, III, however, dashed out of the auto, past his expostulating brother and

sister, and did something. He snatched up the White
Monarch of Glenmere just as Mr. O'Boyle, with a
sneer on his thin lips, allowed the Gas-House Pup to
jerk the leather out of his hand. But, instead of
meeting in the snowy coat of the Monarch, the teeth
of the leaping dog clicked in the air. A quick twist
of the lithe waist of the third Beckwith deHavin had
swung his burden back of him, and the hurtling
brindle-and-white flash carried past, right into the
Monarch's car through the open door, which was
slammed quickly shut, leaving the Grip alone, confounded, and perhaps a little frightened in strange
quarters, somewhat more luxurious than his box of
straw in the Interborough Gas Company's stables.

" 'Beastly cur,' huh?" Mr. Slugs O'Boyle was
snarling into the faces of Miss Audrey and Mr.
Forsythe deHavin, as Mr. A. Beckwith replaced the
squirming Monarch on the sidewalk. "Fat chance
for your white snob to get a champeenship in there
today if I had only turned the 'beastly cur' loose to
pasture on him a second sooner. His champeenship!"
And his mouth went wry with scorn. "Of what? Of
a thousand stalls of milk-fed pussy-hounds. Where
a pit bull, such as is all dog, ain't even allowed to
bench!

"B'Chees, I believe the bunch of you stuffed shirts
is afraid to let your candy pups go up agin a honest
pit terry, even in the show ring, let alone the pit, for
fear the judge would get his eye full wanst of a honest-
to-God dog!"

" 'Beastly cur,' huh?" he repeated, and his lips pulled away from some broken teeth. "Wot's his name? Champeen Pure White Percy'd be my guess. There's just wan place where champeens is made— the pit! And him! In the pit!"

And Mr. Slugs O'Boyle, in his contempt, puckered up his mouth and thrust out his chin toward the spot where the White Monarch of Glenmere was sniffing very doggily at the lower crack of his car door, and looking back questioningly over his shoulder at A. Beckwith deHavin, with that certain uptilt of chin and backroll of eyes which have been patented for bulldoggy use the wide world over.

An ugly stain splashed out on the Monarch's per- fectly groomed coat. Upon which Miss Audrey de- Havin screamed again, horrified: and it was she, this time, who caught up the heavy animal, careless of the moist smear of my Lady Nicotine against the yellow silk of her sport coat.

Mr. Forsythe Wentworth deHavin, true to form, also did something useless.

"I owe your ugly brute an apology, my dear but filthy mucker," said this narrow-chested gentleman. 'I should have called the animal on the other end of your dog's leash a beastly cur."

And he raised his light walking stick backhanded over his shoulder.

Mr. Slugs O'Boyle grinned crooked amusement. He laid the back of his left hand along his right cheek, hunched his broad back, lowered his chin on his chest, and drew back his right arm a trifle. The switching cane would have found only the button of his tight-cap uncovered; and the "counter" trembling in that right arm would have laid Mr. Forsythe Wentworth deHavin on the social shelf for as many weeks as it would have taken his dentist to make up the necessary bridges.

But A. B. deHavin, III, tapped his knuckles briskly on his brother's soft biceps, and the cane fell to the sidewalk.

"You were about to say, when you accidentally spat on my dog—" inquired the third A. Beckwith of Mr. O'Boyle.

"I was sayin', when I spit on your dog—" began Mr. O'Boyle, emphasizing the omission.

"I'm sure you'll pardon my interruption," said Mr. deHavin with utmost suavity; "but you were saying, when you accidentally spat on my dog—" And he reached back into the tail of his coat with a very care-less but deliberate gesture.

Mr. O'Boyle had looked often enough into the eyes of gentlemen in the other corner of the squared circle to be a fair judge of what he saw there. But he looked now into the eyes of the best poker player at the Glen-mere Hunt Club—which, as you may be aware, is not an inconsiderable distinction—and he could learn absolutely nothing in their pale grey depths about the deliberate hand menacing under those immaculate coat tails. It was daylight in the very heart of New York; so surely— But the eyes were hard—very hard.

"When I 'accidently' spit on your dog," repeated Mr. Slugs O'Boyle, putting a contemptuous accent on the word, but using it, nevertheless, "I was sayin' that any champeenship he ever got would last him about three minutes in the pit with the best dog that ever got inside of that gas buggy there."

Mr. A. Beckwith deHavin, III, brought from back of him the threatening handkerchief and flicked various imaginary dog hairs from his coat. Mr. O'Boyle went raw at the thought of what a hand had bluffed him down; and rawer still when, without another word, or so much as another glance, all three aristocratic backs were turned aggravatingly upon him as Mr. deHavin, III, piloted his brother and sister toward one of the Twenty-sixth Street entrances to the Garden.

Going up the steps, Miss Audrey repeated a charming golden display. A door swung wide. Out into the noisy city came a chorus that jerked forward the delicate rose ears of the White Monarch of Glenmere and made him lose all interest in his limousine and what his limousine contained. But the sweet resounding din from a thousand show benches warmed no cockles in the heart of Mr. Slugs O'Boyle. He merely made his final insults more contemptible by calling them to the bulldog instead of to his escort.

"And to get your lickin' wouldn't be so bad, you big white mut!" he said. "The best of dogs and men that ever fights gets licked. But you wouldn't have the guts to lose right."

In another moment the door would close on those

three intolerable backs.   Mr. O'Boyle raised his voice to a shout:

"There never was blue bloods yet, if you put the gaff into 'em, that wouldn't show a damn sight more yellow up their backs than up their legs."

Mr. A. Beckwith de Havin, III, whirled instantly on his heel, his face as purple as his sister's.   He stepped swiftly down to the pavement and flashed a card out of his vest pocket, extending it between two fingers.

"Communicate with me, please," he said very quietly, "whenever it suits you to have your dog try to prove that what you please to term a blue blood can't lose right."   And then he added just as evenly, with never a rise in his tone: "And count on this, please: that if your dog has any convincing arguments I shall be satisfied to let the matter stand as demonstrated; but if not, you will either offer decent apology for your indecent insults or I shall feel obliged to further disprove your theory by personally batting the few teeth the other fellow left for me right down your filthy throat!"

Andrews, the chauffeur, unlatched the door of the deHavin car, and McDonald's Grip, still bewildered by his sudden luxurious imprisonment, nosed Mr. O'Boyle's leg, broke that gentleman's astounded stare toward a closed entrance of the Garden, and proceeded with him out Twenty-sixth Street as far as Lexington Avenue before his trainer realized that the fiercest pit terrier in America was travelling New York's streets with a training leash.

Glenmere White Monarch proceeded to his bench, pawed his way clumsily onto it, received a touch of soapy cloth, towel and talcum on a stained spot over his shoulder, shook an ingratiating paw stiff-leggedly with as many visitors as knew how different was his disposition from his style of beauty, and finally proceeded to the winners' ring, where, scoring over the old campaigner, Champion Forrest Hills Kennels Penfold Cavalier, in sourness of expression only, he took, nevertheless, the blue, and the five points he needed to give him the coveted prefix, Ch.

II

Mr. Patrick O'Boyle was, both naturally and by consistent effort, as different from his brother Terrance, better known to fame as Slugs, as he could possibly be.

Mr. Terrance O'Boyle's forehead was low. His hair was bristly black. His eyes were close. His lips were thin. His body was bovine, his nose broken, and his ears cauliflower.

Mr. Patrick O'Boyle had a fair, broad brow, crowned thickly with a curly dark-red thatch. His eyes set out on the edges of his face. His mouth smiled steadily such a Celtic breadth that it threatened the location of his ears. And these ears had been, up to this time, too cleverly protected to allow any five-ounce glove, full of knuckles, to break their gristle. His nose, too, had shared this same impenetrable defence, for it still uptilted in ancient and undamaged

Erse impertinence above the long upper lip. And as for muscular action, the movements of Brother Pat partook of none of the bull-like strength of Brother Terrance. Let it rather be said in description that a young tiger, by minding his step, could no doubt have moved his body every bit as easily and as wickedly swift as could KO Pat O'Boyle.

Also, Patrick's body was scrupulously clean from heel to head outside, and from skin to skin inside—muscle, tendon, blood, nerve, bone and marrow—and, therefore, matched his immortal soul. The soul of the other Brother O'Boyle was also a fit tenant for its house; which need not necessarily be construed as a compliment, for Brother Terrance had no special enthusiasm for Saturday evening, on which day he followed the time-honoured custom of performing certain rites deemed necessary only in connection with donning Sunday attire. And as for internal cleanliness, he had ceased even his ill-spirited training after the old third-rater trial-horse heavy, Jim Flint, had bounced a hay-maker off the point of his jaw.

As to the point of material prosperity, Mr. Terrance was not what might be termed an object of envy, for his present position in the world of affairs was that of trainer of Shamus McDonald's stable of fighting dogs; while at the moment of our introduction to Brother KO Pat we find him surrounded by a circle of reporters, backers, trainers, managers, gamblers, true sportsman followers of the Game, and friends; among whom could be numbered, as belonging to the last two classes, a tall, dapper, well-knit young fellow, caned and monocled to extinction, pale yellow of hair and tintless of skin, but with light eyes whose grey sparkle belied the general pallor of his colouring; which same young swell answered in this company to the seemingly appropriate name of Becky.

"Now throw in high, the bunch of you," grinned Pat O'Boyle after a quarter hour of the usual after-training chatter; "for I'll not be answerin' foolish question No. 31569 today, and I'll be makin' no statements as to how I'm going to lay Stinger Wilson away before the sixth. You reportin' lads can easy enough write out a column or two of that con without any help from me." And he unceremoniously shooed out of his training quarters all but his very closest friend, who proved to be the pale-haired Becky mentioned before.

"Do I know anything about McDonald's Grip?" repeated Mr. O'Boyle. "Do I know the Gas-House Pup? You don't happen to know the maiden name of Mrs. Patrick O'Boyle, I guess. Well, I'll be tellin' it to you when I say that Old Shamus McDonald is the whitest, squarest old sport of a daddy-in-law that any lad ever crowed about. And McDonald's Grip is as white and square as his master, and can go twice as far in a ruction; which is such high praise as could only be said of the best pit terrier in the world—which he is. And more than that, for that doggie has brought out the only love that evei showed through the black heart of his trainer, which same is my own blackguard brother, Terry. Why do you ask?"

"Only because a short, broad, red-faced, white-haired gentleman, who, no doubt, is this same daddy-in-law, came shouldering into our drawing-room last evening, a-bouncing our protesting Jephcott backward off his chest at every step, and presented me with one of my own cards, and wanted to know, first, if I was the son of my dad; and, second, if he might be allowed the courtesy of looking over the White Monarch; and, third, when it would suit me to match the dogs."

"Match what dogs?" growled Mr. O'Boyle sceptically.

"Grip and the Monarch."

Patrick O'Boyle let out a whoop that would have graced the liveliest ruction at an ancient Donegal Fair.

"For the worship of my good name saint!" he yelled, and ducked back under the shower as though to revive his fainting spirits.

He gave the faucet handle a fling wide over to the cold-water side of the valve. A moment later, standing widelegged in dripping and superb unconscious nakedness before Mr. Becky deHavin, he addressed that gentleman vehemently, emphasizing his remarks by waving a wetter and wetter towel under the aristocratic nose.

"You don't mean to stand there in front of me, without your guard up, and tell me you're gonna put the Monarch into the pit with the Gas-House Pup!" he shouted.

Becky deHavin nodded affirmation.

"But—hell's bells!—Becky, me boy, if he could come out of it with no more than a slit ear he'd be done on the bench forever. And him with a Garden best-of-the-breed win tacked onto him at the beginning of his career!"

"But I had to do it, Pat. A beast who had Grip on the lead said that the Monarch couldn't lose right. And that there never was a blue blood that could. And then the skunk passed an insulting remark that brought my sister rudely into our street brawl. There are times, friend Pat, when a man and his dog have simply got to fight."

"True for you," sanctioned Mr. O'Boyle; "and specially if it's my hard brother's ugly sneer that goes with the words; and I seem to see his fine Irish hand at work in this. But do you know what it means when the gang at the pit says a dog's 'lost right'? Here's what it means: that when it comes his turn to scratch, no matter how he's torn and weak, or how many of his legs is broke, or how many hours he has stood up under the teeth of a better dog, just the same he carries the fight across into the other corner of the pit, without a stop or a pause, if he has to crawl every inch of the way to his beatin' flat on his belly. A dog or man, or any other fightin' animal, loses when he quits, and a pit dog that loses right quits when he's dead."

KO O'Boyle's eyes were full of accusation.

"Sure, you don't want the old friend dog to come to an end like that!" he said.

"I think the old Jerrypups might prefer just that

kind of an end," replied Becky. "I believe he'd rather round the Horn, if he had his choice, in the strength of his youth and the joy of death grips that to have me end the suffering of old and worn-out days by holding the cone down tight over his feebly protesting nose."

DeHavin's eyes went hot at the thought of the hour that comes to all who have had a dog for a friend. Then he applied his handkerchief to his nose—a little high perhaps—and said:

"And, on the other hand, why assume that he's going to lose?"

"Undershot!" explained O'Boyle, dismissing the possibility of a win with that one word. "I'm tellin' you 'tis a damn shame to be putting a white wonder like the Monarch onto the tan-bark with Grip. If it was only the spoiling of all them thousands of dollars' worth of dog, I'd not be kicking to you; for a good scrap's worth whatever you can afford to pay for it. But this won't be good. There won't be no fight. It ain't treatin' the Monarch fair; for he won't have the chance of that old cotton cat."

"Why not?"

"His jaw! He ain't made for the game. He's lived too easy—him and his ancestors. The fighting days of his breed is hundreds of years in the past. Why, I'll bet you my winnings with Stinger that you won't even be able to make old Monarch train."

Mr. Becky deHavin smiled superior knowledge. He switched his light cane to and fro complacently.

"Train?" he said. "Why, the old Monarch is fit to go to the mat this minute with any dog, wild cat or elephant in the country. There's not an ounce of fat on him. While getting him in shape for the Hunt Club's outdoor show, where he made his last killing, I walked him five miles up hill and down dale every day for a month."

Patrick Aloysius O'Boyle gazed into his friend's monocle in despair. "Five miles a day!" he roared. "Duck your nut!"

A. Beckwith ducked it. A soggy towel, bundled into a heavy wad, flew over his head and banged against the wall.

"All of that?" KO Patrick exploded derisively. "And you're the man that's going to put your good dog into the pit with McDonald's Grip? Considerin' his fondness for bones, you ought to let the Monarch nibble on your head a while. Five miles! Well, I'll be damned!"

Mr. O'Boyle paused for breath and surveyed his pale-haired friend witheringly before he went at him again.

"Listen to common sense!" he said. "I'm trainin' for ten rounds, or as much less as it'll take me to drop Stinger Wilson into the garbage can—thirty minutes actual work, with ten minutes' rest divided among the thirty. But I go out that damn sand road that far and back again every morning to earn my breakfast— a little starter for the day's work. If you got brains, now use them: In his last fight it took the Gas-House

Pup three hours and twenty-seven minutes to kill Gallivan's Slasher Bill."

Becky deHavin's delicate pale face showed the dawning of grave comprehension.

"All right, Pat," he said. "I guess I've been miscalculating the size of the Monarch's job."

"I thought I could show you it was the right thing to call it off," said Pat.

"Call what off?" snapped Becky deHavin. "Both I and the Monarch have been living too easy. We're going to work. He's got a theory to disprove; and I've contracted with you to help me train to trim a man twice my weight, who probably is your brother. When do we start the grind?"

Patrick O'Boyle saw in the pale eyes the kind of fire that he knew meant trouble when he saw it gleaming in the opposite corner of the ring.

"Today," said KO Pat. "And because I'm foolish fond of the two of you I'm gonna work you till you holler for mercy."

III

Late on a sunny afternoon a month after the meeting of Mr. Slugs O'Boyle with the scions of the House of deHavin, a lacquered palace, built on pneumatic foundations—a sort of castle on air, as it were—floated to a stop in front of the training quarters of KO Pat O'Boyle, challenger for the world's lightweight title; and two elderly gentlemen disembarked. The stout pale gentleman, with the shell-rimmed glasses and the grouch, was none other than Mr. A. Beckwith deHavin, II, president and general manager of the Interborough Gas Company, himself; and the stout florid gentleman, without any glasses at all, and a smile, was none other than Mr. Shamus McDonald, P. and G. M. of the Interborough Gas Company's stables, himself.

The grouch and the smile linked arms, and sallied up the steps to the entrance of the long and high-fenced yard that reached from the motor drive to the Hudson.

"What newspaper?" asked a young man who affected the habiliments of his calling—heelless ring shoes; wide-cuffed peg trousers; and a high-necked, long-sleeved jersey, tucked down shirt-fashion inside a belt which was rendered superfluous by the flaunting suspenders that topped his sweater. A cap of generous size completed the towel-swinger's uniform; and this was cocked sidewise and yanked down tight from the back of the neck to where the pouch of the long peak was stretched down to his eyebrows; and it added just the bellicose touch necessary to elicit a pugnacious reply from Mr. deHavin, II.

"Newspaper—hell!" responded that gentleman. "Do these two fronts look as though they belonged to a couple of half-starved cubs?"

"Big belly or small," shot back the suspenders, "they don't come busting in on Mr. O'Boyle's afternoon nap unless they show me first."

"Which means," grinned Shamus McDonald at his boss appreciatively, "that you send in your card and cool your heels in the lobby for a while, gettin' a taste of your own medicine thereby."

"You'd think he was a hundred-thousand-dollar-a year man," blustered Mr. deHavin.

"He will be that, and more, the minute he hangs a KO on Stinger Wilson's jaw," said Shamus McDonald proudly. Then: "Here, son,"—to the lilac-suspendered Cerberus—"lean that tin ornament over to me." And he whispered a few words in his ear.

Upon which a wide gleam of teeth opened up under the long-peaked cap, and with all affability he ushered the two stout gentlemen into the sacred sleeping presence of KO Pat.

"What's· the open-sesame, Shamus?" asked Mr. de-Havin.

"What's the what?" said Shamus.

It happened that, at the time the visitors entered, Mr. O'Boyle was not, as was his usual custom at this time of day, enjoying a well-earned siesta under the little canvas that was spread down by the springing board at the wharf, but was hanging over a low fence that inclosed one corner of the tráining camp. On one side of him the second A. Beckwith deHavin recognized the supple shoulders and pale-yellow hair of the third of that same name. On the other side of Mr. O'Boyle there leaned a purple bathrobe, out of the top of which poked a rubber bathing cap of tan, and under the skirt of which appeared a pleasant project of neatest bathing slippers and light-brown, bare, slender ankles.

Age had not dimmed the eye of the second A. B. deHavin; and immediately a suspicion came into his mind that boxing lessons, the training of Glenmore White Monarch, and a true friendship for Pat O'Boyle, the man, were not the three only attractions that brought the pale blond Beckwith out to the fighter's quarters daily.

Inside the fence on which the trio leaned their elbows stood a centre upright post of four-by-four timber, some eight feet high, guyed at the top through a bearing and seated at the bottom in a socket. Extending from a point near the bottom of the four-by-four, two horizontal two-by-fours, braced to the upright, extended radially ten or twelve feet, until they were a considerable distance apart at the ends. A beaten tan-bark path marked a circle about the upright as a center, with the horizontal timbers as radii.

And, lying flat on his stomach, tethered back and front between the ends of the radial two-by-fours, with forelegs stretched out in front and back legs stretched out full length flat behind him, frog-fashion, lay the panting form of the White Monarch of Glenmore. His tongue hung out for yards and yards and dripped a clear and healthy saliva as he perspired there. And his sweet brown eyes, with never a move of his recumbent head, rolled toward the three who stood there trying to wheedle him into further revolutions in his training machine.

"This is my good friend Pat O'Boyle, governor," said the young deHavin as his father and the smiling McDonald came up to the fence. "And this is my daddy, Nora—father, Miss McDonald."

Nora McDonald held her purple bathrobe close about her with one hand and put the other one out to the senior deHavin. It didn't look exactly like the hand of a stable boss's daughter; in fact, it was a better-looking hand than the daughter of the stable boss's boss could have shown. Not any softer to be sure, but just as soft—and firmer in the grasp; and a beautiful live brown instead of a dead white; and a little rounder and a bit more shapely. All of which A. B. deHavin, II, noticed as he held it. A. B. de-Havin, III, had inherited all his noticing abilities—which were acute.

"I'm mighty glad to meet a daughter of Shamus McDonald," said the president of the Interborough Gas Company, "but I'm very sure, Shamus, that I've met your girl somewhere before. Her face is mighty familiar. Do you remember our ever meeting, Miss McDonald? I'm both ashamed of and astounded at myself for not recalling where."

And he took a fine big look at her, ostensibly to assist his recollection; maybe for other reasons best known to himself. At any rate, the pale eyes of A. B. the third took on a twinkle; and, apropos of nothing whatever, he said: "Dad, you'll have to buy a ticket for that."

Nora McDonald's eyes sparkled, also.

"Perhaps you will recall me when you see more of me," she said.

At this a grin broke out that was shared by all present but the senior A. B.

Not being in on the laugh brought Father deHavin's ever-ready grouch blooming into view.

"Well," he asked his son, "do you you think that dog is going to get into shape for the Gas-House Pup by laying there on his stomach? How many minutes did he do to-day?"

"Fifteen."

"Fifteen, huh!" retorted father and grouch in unison. "The only part of the training that you seem to be able to make that dog do thoroughly is to take his alcoholic rub and eat his five pounds of beef rump daily. You made the match that's going to ruin him for the bench if he doesn't get killed; and I'm putting it up to you to have him right. I want at least one member of the family that I needn't be ashamed to put up against a scrap. Get this accomplished at least —I haven't asked you to do anything else, so far, have I?"

The pale eyes of the third A. Beckwith deHavin shot the same fire that came out of them when he put on the ten-ounce gloves with an erstwhile and future friend named Pat O'Boyle. When they flew at each other in their training bouts, if any friendship lived on then, it was invisible to the naked eye. Had not the presence of the girl restricted the flow of language that rose to his lips, he might have relieved the pressure that made his colourless skin glow red. As it was, he mastered his tongue in gentlemanly fashion and blushed out his embarrassment with only a few low-spoken words.

"Why *don't* you ask me to?" he said.

But Shamus McDonald broke in with a word:

"Let's not go to war about this," said he. "As I've insisted many times since the match was made, let's call the ruction off. Never would I have been a party to it, anyhow, if I had looked at the bulldog's fangs when I first went out to see him. No matter what's his condition and courage, the fight's not goin' to be a fair one unless your dog can punish; and that he can't. We'll call it quits."

But the hard look was still in the eyes of Becky deHavin.

"He'll do his other ten minutes in the trainer," said that young man. "He's done his schedule every day, so far; though it does take a bit of persuasion." He scowled squarely at his father, with a look that returned his grouch with interest; then turned and glared at Shamus McDonald. "And there'll be no more talk about calling quits. I don't like the word."

Then he spoke to McDonald's daughter; and the scowl vanished, and the grey glint melted to an altogether different colour in his eyes:

"Will you help me with him, Miss McDonald?"

Now the training of a pit dog is almost a cruel thing. For a month before his fight he walks and runs interminably. He worries a coonskin, tied to the end of a heavy flexible sapling that springs with his weight and the pull of a rope in his trainer's hand, till at times he is flipped back somersaulting off his feet. He works with this endlessly, till his eye grows accurate and his jaws become perfect to strike the snapping skin; and he learns to hold his grip, and to switch his body back and forth with bone-breaking force by the play of his powerful neck thews.

But the grind that tries the heart and patience of the most courageous dogs is the daily monotony of the training machine. Ten minutes, fifteen minutes, twenty, twenty-five, thirty, thirty-five—the daily drag increases until the poor dog thinks he shall never cease his endless circling round the sawdust path. Cajoled, bullied, scolded, bribed, punished by all methods but those that would tend to break his spirit, he does his allotted daily bit; and the discipline of it gets to be part of him. As he learns that he must stand up under long and punishing work, the heart to endure the bitter hours through which he may have to stand his beating in the pit grows sturdy within him; and, along with the fiery joy of perfect health and strength and dazzling speed, comes the power to endure under monotonous suffering—and endure—and endure—and endure; which is the true measure of all kinds of strength.

And the good-natured, lazy, lovable White Monarch of Glenmere was puzzled and annoyed at the necessity for leaving off his days of splendid indolence at the Glenmere Hunt Club Kennels for the rigours of the training camp of Pat O'Boyle. But by rapid degrees he came to enjoy that part of his work which had the zest of sport in it. He fairly revelled in his daily boxing bout with KO Pat. Again and again and again he would charge into the blows of the boxer's padded fists. Knocked head over heels, end over end, into the sawdust, he would scramble savagely to his feet again and, with a lion's growl rumbling in his throat, fly into the whizzing gloves with a speed and craft which increased so rapidly day by day that the time soon came when he could bull his way occasionally through the accurate blows into the padded sweater. Then a twist of his thick neck muscles would lash the fifty pounds of his body back and forth till the fabric yielded and the sweater was ripped from top to bottom. So fierce and swift became this romp that it soon began to help the eye and speed of Pat O'Boyle; and the stopping of those snarling charges had no ill effect on the boxer's courage, albeit the short tail wagged and wagged throughout the game.

But if some mysterious reason had not arisen for Miss Nora McDonald to pay very frequent visits to her sister, and so to spend much time practising her twenty-five beautiful dives off the wharf of her brother-in-law's training camp, it is doubtful if the White Monarch could ever have been compelled to forego his hatred for the training machine. But the Irish girl was the one who discovered his almost hysterical fondness for the water. And now, at young Mr. de-

Havin's request, she used again the bribe she had found would work on the Monarch.

"Jerry go swim?" she asked.

Ears up.

"Go swim?" she wheedled again.

The panting dog was on his feet, eyes bright, head tilted to one side, tail so close to being gay that, had he ever elevated it to such a height in the judging ring, he might never have affixed the Ch. to his name.

"All right! Go swim," she said again, and started toward the wharf and the springing board that stood at the river end of the camp.

And good old Jerrydog, knowing from previous lessons that he should get no water romp unless he completed his task in the machine, started briskly to complete the deadly grind; and so plodded his unhappy way about and about, dragging the cursed lumber back of him, pushing ahead of him the devilish scantling that he could never overtake, until at last the voice he loved best in the world said to him, "That's a *good* dog!" Thus the gentle big bulldog learned that at the end of every long and honest fatigue there was a reward; and a white streak heads for the river.

On the wharf a purple bathrobe drops away, and a brown one-piece—one very small piece—diving suit shows how daringly near a match can be made between tan silk and tanned skin—and many other altogether charming things. An undulating stride or two and a slim brown figure hits the end of the springing board and rises almost perpendicularly into the air, hands up, back arched; and then, without any motion below the waist, bends double till finger tips touch instep. At the very top of the rise the slim legs snap up, stiff-kneed, feet pointed, and the low flat curves drop plumb into the water two feet from the end of the board in a perfect jackknife, splashless, like a hot knife into butter. And up on the wharf and out over the springing board in a flying leap the joyous bulldog streaks, and disappears with a splash. Then the white head and the tan one come to the surface together, and there starts that romping hour of the day for which both of them live.

The moment the brown jackknife opened its delicious blade a chuckle broke its way through the senior deHavin's grouch.

"When I see more of her!" he snorted appreciatively. 'So one of the Hawaiian Diving Twins is Miss Nora McDonald! And who, I wonder, will the other of the Kolananikau Sisters prove to be?"

"Who else but Mrs. Kate O'Boyle?" asked KO Pat with an entirely pardonable pride. "Who will not be showin' in vodvil with her sister this winter on account of a more important season's contract she has on her hands."

And Messrs. McDonald and O'Boyle beamed on each other pompously, as though some new thing had come to pass under the sun.

IV

Miss Audrey deHavin protested.

"But, papa," she said, accenting the proper syllable of the paternal title—"a diving girl!"

"Not at all; not at all, Audrey," reassured papa as he folded his napkin and took a cigar from the tray that Jephcott was stiff-arming out to him. *"The* diving girl!" And he looked mildly round his family circle. "At fifteen hundred a week!"—as though he would by no means omit a fact of so great importance.

"Mrs. A. Beckwith deHavin, son and daughter." he continued, "if Beckwith wants to marry Nora McDonald he's got a lot better sense than I ever suspected. And if he can win her he's a lot better son than I had any notion was in our family; and Papa deHavin isn't going to disown him if he does it. If you insist, I might threaten disinheritance—just to help matters along; but I'd like to see if he has sense enough to pick out a woman instead of a doll to marry, without the urge of parental opposition. I should like, more than I can say, to see one of my offspring do something. And if my batting eye is still as good as I think it is the winning of Nora McDonald is that."

"But, Beckwith, dear"—Mother deHavin employed that tone of finality which had closed innumerable family debates in her favour—"she is the daughter of your stable foreman!"

"And a damn fine foreman, at that!" said Papa de-

Havin; and Jephcott turned what would have been an inexcusable gasp into a cough, and dropped the cigar tray. "And she has a prize-fighting brother-in-law she'll be proud to introduce to the family."

The family's gasp far, far outshone the butler's very best accomplishment.

"At one hundred thousand a year," added papa, again as though he attached much importance to such information.

It is not improbable that to Papa deHavin such round, mouth-filling figures suggested accomplishment; and accomplishment was not the middle name of any of those who sat at table with Papa deHavin that evening.

As Papa deHavin continued to talk, an unknown speaker appeared suddenly before his family; and the family dropped its several jaws and listened to him.

"Shamus McDonald, my extra fine stable boss," began this stranger, "looked at our bulldog the other day and said this to me: 'Your dog is going to lose right, boss. I guess it's in a straight breed to lose right when the big call comes. Ain't it a terrible pity he can't win! But he can't; he's too white—the fighting brindle's all bred out of him.'

"Now look at all of us." Papa deHavin arraigned his startled audience under his famous grouch. "We're getting paler-coloured every day. I want a son to run the Interborough, and haven't got one brindle enough. I believe, with Shamus, that even Forsythe there, who is perhaps the most worthless of us all, would lose right. He'd take his beating like a man if the big call came. But that's not getting me the natural winning fighter I've got to have to make the Interborough a winning gas company. My offspring are all too white. For the sake of type, the brindle's all been bred out. *I'm* slipping. I'm showing the downward trend. Here I am, looking for a son to turn over my business to at fifty-seven. Great-grandad deHavin was still breaking harness at eighty-five. I've some hopes for Becky; but if he's good he'll be our last good one, unless we breed in some of the fighting brindle. And I'm not going to stop any one who tries to shoot into the deHavin veins some new, red yeoman blood. Does everybody get me?"

Everybody got him.

Bull deHavin, so known among his friends and enemies downtown—who believed, as many others of his kind believe, in being Papa deHavin after half-past hour, even at many sacrifices of ideals and desires—had appeared once, famous grouch in hand, in the bosom of his family, at a crisis; had bellowed a few times, tossed his horns once or twice, and then disappeared forever, metaphorically pawing up the plush rugs of home with a certain secret satisfaction as he stamped back into the fens and fastnesses of the Interborough Gas Company.

Jephcott at last recovered his equilibrium sufficiently to recover the cigar tray; then, with his usual *savoir-faire*, hurried out into the hall for what he thought was necessary to relieve the situation. And when his back was turned to the family a smile of approbation, marvellous to behold, split wide the mask of inhuman imperturbability that ordinarily answered for his face.

True to form, young Mr. Forsythe Wentworth, trying to lessen the tension, put his foot in it up to his waist.

"Since Beckwith cannot go with us tonight, papa," he said mildly, subtly changing the conversation's drift, "suppose you help to fill our box. Caruso sings Pagliacci tonight."

Jephcott handed Papa deHavin his hat and stick.

"Palyach the wart on your grandmother's nose, Forsythe!" Papa fired a parting shot from the doorway.

"Becky nd I will be together tonight—in attendance at a man's entertainment. We're going to a dog fight."

v

The pit was a very silent, ominous, bright-yellow square, surrounded on all sides by whispering darkness; small—less than three paces on a side; and the low-hung lamps glaring upon it made its surroundings dim and indistinct. Sloping up back of the glare of the lights, there rose a bank of glowing sparks, where the burning tobacco of men ran high into the smoke-laden gloom. Long wisps of the reek undulated gracefully under the lighted hoods. A hush that was not altogether precaution against police interference hung heavily, as though to usher in some deed of awe.

More than a thousand men sat, whispering, waiting in the shadow back of the low pit fence; for in the old days of the dog-fighting game the name of Grip, the Gas-House Pup, would fill whatever enclosure staged the fight.

And this night Grip was matched against the menacing unknown—against a dog with, back of him, the legendry of that inexhaustible supply of courage to which could be traced the valour of all the fighting breeds, but which had not known the fighting game since the long years past, when his ancestors had been matched against the savagest bulls of Britain. Had the indomitable bravery lasted through? Would it come out? Or was the tradition of the unbreakable heart of the pure bulldog nothing but a myth—or built upon absolute fact? Had the ancient bullbaiters, when they bred his nose back so that he might breathe while his whole face was buried in the dewlap of the bull, overdone their work, and ruined him for self-protection against attacks of his own kind? These were questions the visible answering of which would have filled Madison Square Garden, had the authorities allowed, with a crowd which would have made the attendance at the annual bench classic in that same edifice look small and apathetic.

And that other question, eternal and momentous among men: Was there one created living thing that had no quitting point? And was that thing the bulldog? To the cock fighters assembled there the dog men whispered their ancient answers: that the dog was a thinking animal, and that the gamecock would fight to the death only with his own kind; while there had not yet been discovered on the earth any created thing that the bulldog—bless his gentle heart!—could not be prevailed upon to tackle. Battle to the death did not answer that question, anyhow. Hardly a man gathered there but had seen more than one pit dog lose his battle "right"; but the question still remained unsolved: Did he quit the struggle just before he died —or afterward? Could he have lasted longer, would he finally have reached the point where he could have forced his noble heart to endure no more?

This mystery, however unsolvable, from the very nature of it, in this world, was strong in collecting these hard men into the gloom round that sinister yellow square. How could any bulldog, however nobly bred and grandly made, discover that awful secret? And yet, for the first time in pit history a man had been found rich enough in purse and sporting blood to put a bulldog, with an invaluably long and spotless pedigree, to the test. Many things might be learned before that fight was over. And the whisperings died to bated silence as young Becky deHavin, immaculate in evening attire, came striding across the yellow square.

His face was somewhat drawn, as it might have looked had a dear friend's life been hanging in the balance. He extended his hand out of the light to where his father and Shamus McDonald and Pat O'Boyle were seated together, at the shadow's edge.

"Mr. McDonald," he said in a low voice that reached every strained pair of ears in the whole house, "I want to try to thank you, and Miss McDonald through you, for your help in training Jerry, and for your advice as regards handling him here. I've never met with higher sportsmanship."

Shamus McDonald took hearty hold of the hand.

"What credit for the Grip to stop a dog that's not trained for the gaff or that hasn't a handler for him to fall back on in the pit here? Get hustling back to your pup before somebody slips a hypodermic into him."

" 'Tis a dirty game," said Shamus McDonald to the elder deHavin and O'Boyle as the young man hurried away, "and I'm goin' to quit it."

Pit men seated close about the dean of the dog-fighting game overheard him, and the whisper of it soon reached the farthest corners of the audience. Most men smiled incredibly; but those who were his friends, and therefore white men, shook their heads as though they understood, and spoke gloomily about the future of the savage sport.

"It's no fit game for you and me to play," continued McDonald. "For look—here's you and me, who'd rather lose a leg than play it dirty—and our two dogs being tasted this very minute."

"Tasted?" asked the senior deHavin.

"In days gone by 'twas the right word; for then your opponent's man rubbed moist fingers through your dog's coat and actually licked them for traces of dope that might fix his own dog. Nowadays both dogs are washed under the other party's watch—the washing to get rid of any poison on their coats; the watching to see that the washer doesn't slip the dog a pill, or pour a few birdshot in his ear, or shoot him with the needle under the washwater in the tub. A hundred visitors at your kennels, a hundred visitors at mine, and a score of trainers, handlers and seconds, all have their dirty money placed so many ways that you can trust no one in the pit; and this thing is getting worse from year to year. Too many see only the money and none of the glory in a dog fight and I'm gonna quit the game."

And he did. That night's fight was the last one in which Shamus McDonald ever fought a dog. There never lived a greater lover of dogs. He never fought one that did not love the game better than his master. His heart broke when he lost his pets in the pit; but he thought that, given their choice, they would have asked him to be allowed to come to their end in the rapture of deadly combat. Shamus McDonald's dogs were that kind of dogs. But Shamus McDonald, and other white men after him, dropped the pit game; and it died, as all games die, in time, that cannot be kept clean. And so the brutal, savage, bloody entertainments stopped, which, but for insidious practice, might have lasted to this day. For what two dogs join issues on the street today but that a crowd well nigh impenetrable and wholly masculine gathers in a forward-bent ring to watch even such untrained and inexperienced grappling; and departs with many a re-gretful growl when a master, or some officious stranger stops the undecided fray.

And now the quiet deepened about the yellow square, for handlers, trainers, attendants and officials came straddling over the pit fence, out of the shadow into the glare; and carefully wrapped and blanketed bundles, carried in the arms of two of the men, drew all eyes to the two corners, where these wriggling packages were set on the ground.

Dapper Becky deHavin, coached in the dirty trick-eries of the game by his opponent, walked beside the man who carried his dog, holding his hands over the black nose that poked out of the squirming blanket, keeping the ears down tight; never taking his hands away from the broad muzzle till the Monarch was on the floor and the blanket off, and all chance of under-hand work reduced to a minimum.

A gasp of surprise and delight came out of the smoke. Perhaps there was even a little of awe in the involuntary tribute. Hardly a man there who did not know the superb Grip, peer of all fighting dogs—hardly a man to whom the brindled body and blazed face, and the snowy full-dress collar and shirt bosom, and four white feet, were not a familiar and magnifi-cent sight. And the splendid, living muscles of him never slipped beneath that scarred brindle hide more tigerishly lithe than on that night. But the indrawn breath of a thousand hard men was not a tribute to the Gas-House Dog; for in the opposite corner to him a blanket whisked away and discovered such a bulldog as neither show ring nor pit had ever seen before.

Dazzling white was the whole of him in the lamps' bright glare. Remained on his mighty body not a trace of the ancient mastiff brindle that had come to be a colour dreaded by the bare-calved legions of Rome in the days when his wild forbears had fought at the side of the wilder British tribesmen. Pear-shaped was he—the heavy end of the fruit the tremendous brisket, which dipped so low inside the wide-spread forelegs that it appeared as though swung between and not supported on them. And those sturdy front limbs went straight to the ground, with never the sign of a bow, like little marble columns. The small end of the pear, the hindquarters, narrowed marvellously at the loins, the top arched up distinctly higher than the shoulders in a beautiful roach; the belly tucked up tight beneath; the back of him so narrow that he seemed to be supported at three points instead of four. Never was there such a model of uncompromising and immovable stability as this low, squat, canine battleship. And the sinews of him bulged gloriously, with never a muscle-bound lump or knot, but in huge, smooth, swelling mounds beneath the loose and roomy skin.

But, in spite of the fascination of every dread-nought line of the wide low mass of his body, his headpiece was such a thing as to make men nearly forget that there was any more dog behind it. A study of absolute perfection in massive ferociousness it was, to cause the most inured pit follower to catch his breath. In size enormous, so that none but masto-donic neck thews could hold it up. The skull was ponderous; wide and long and flat, with something snakelike in the contour of it; and the inky nose was set up tight against the almost negligible brow. And, sweeping up from the dewlapped throat to meet black upper lips that went out almost horizontally an inch or so beyond the nose, the prodigious under jaw curved in a wide, loose-jowled line of power and savagery and stubborn wickedness. When his deli-cately folded ears jerked up on top of his head, alert-ness and truculent readiness radiated from his face; but when they were laid back, close against the thick bull neck, there was added to his belligerent aspect a look of such indescribable meanness that the backers of the Grip shifted uneasily in their seats. And the wide-set eyes spat wicked fires out of their beautiful clear brown. Who could imagine that in that very incarnation of ruthless battle strength there lived a heart as gentle as a little child's?

Back of the shield of his handlers, so that the Grip could get no chance to size up his enemy, Becky deHavin walked his beloved bulldog up and down, and—impossible as it seemed—the moment he moved, all the impression of the animal's power and vigour and intrepidity was immediately doubled; for he trotted back and forth with that stiff-legged swash-buckling roll and captivating swagger which makes his breed win into human hearts at a glance. And as he went his muscles leaped and played. A back view of him showed his two hind legs trotting along close together; but the front stilts, with a jaunty flip of paws, moved clear to the sight far out on each side beyond his flanks. And from this interesting prospect could be discovered, at last, the only place where the good nature of the lovable beast broke through its warlike investure; for the small, low-set tail wigwagged continuous messages of camaraderie up to his boss.

"Make ready!"

The square cleared, except for the two handlers and the referee. Becky deHavin went across the pit and took the Grip between his legs. Midway he met Mr. Slugs O'Boyle, crossing in the opposite direction to observe his part of the pit precaution that makes opponents loose each other's dogs at the beginning of the fight. And a look passed between the burly pugilist and the dapper swell that made the audience gloat. It was to be, also, a battle of handlers in type as different from each other as were their dogs.

A grim silence, such as should precede a battle to the death, fell like a dreadful canopy over the pit.

Becky deHavin's spiketail coat hung over the low fence. Habitual evening formality was not his only reason for his incongruous attire. As he crouched behind the Monarch's deadly enemy the white square of his shirt made a very beacon for his dog across the square.

"Let go!"

Becky deHavin could no more help caressing the wonderful brindle beast that stepped out in front of him than he could have foregone to touch his glove against Pat O'Boyle's at the start of each of their wicked bouts.

Out from between the knees of Slugs O'Boyle, across the pit, stepped sixty pounds of perfect bulldog flesh.

"Come on and get 'im, Jerrypup!" coaxed the low voice that he loved.

And he wagged the only amiable part of him and took another doubtful step toward the middle of the pit, cocking his tremendous head in puzzled inquiry as to just where he should come and whom he should get. Then he spied the white shirtfront.

But for a thing that had never happened before, the fangs of the Gas-House Dog had been locked in his flesh long before now. For the first time in his career the Grip hesitated before he dashed into battle. What kind of dog was this great beast across from him? Where was the other pit terrier? In all his stormy existence he had never faced anything like this dazzling snowy dog that made no offer to attack him. Grip lifted an inquiring eye to Slugs O'Boyle and asked him what about this strange new kind of opponent?

"That's him," explained his handler.

To any who might have entertained the thought that at last too great a call had been made upon the inexhaustible supply of the Grip's pluck, there came a sudden change of heart. True to his traits, Glenmere White Monarch, advancing toward the gleaming front of Becky deHavin's shirt, at sight of the other dog turned to a little Parian statue where he stood; and, standing thus, his slow brain working out the situation, a brindled thunderbolt, hardly more than half his size, fell on him. It was the first fight of the Monarch's life; and it was for this reason only that he committed the one offence of that titanic battle. Taken by surprise by the attack launched on him so suddenly, the whole trend of affairs not yet clear in his mind, he turned a shoulder to the charging Grip.

"That turn," said Shamus McDonald, out of his perfect knowledge of what was going on before him, "is going to lose the scrap for you."

But A. Beckwith deHavin, II, staring tensely out of the shadow, had his eyes fixed not on the bulldog at that moment, but at the trim, white-shirt-sleeved, pale young man moving coolly and efficiently about the whirling brutes.

The Grip was now clamped fast to the side of the Monarch's throat. Well for the bulldog that he had in generous portion the dewlap of his breed, else the Grip had struck him vitally at the first onset. But the long jaws of the terrier filled with folds on folds of the loose skin and his fangs sought in vain for the life that flowed in the throat beneath. He tried at once the first trick of his trade; and, bracing his legs wide, he gave a toss of his head that would have turned another dog all four legs up beneath him, so

"—and he wagged the only amiable part of him and took another doubtful step toward the middle of the pit, cocking his tremendous head in puzzled inquiry."

that he could have tried for a death-hold with a
loosening of his jaws and a new snap of his fangs
before his opponent could turn over and get out from
under him. Now the surge of his neck muscles only
flipped his own hind quarters in the air. He had met
with a new thing. The huge body of the Monarch
was set upon colossal forelegs twice as wide apart as
those of any other dog the Grip had ever closed with;
so, jerk and fling as the maddened brindle might, the
stout white stilts only dragged stiffly about and would
not be uptilted.

"Some wheel base, Becky!" roared the joyful bull
voice of Papa deHavin; and a warning "S-sh!" went
up from the entire audience. No police interference
should stop so great a combat if strained silence could
keep the authorities unaware of it.

"Easy! Easy, boy!" coached a low voice as Becky
deHavin stepped about the struggling animals, keeping
in a position where his dog could see him all the
while. "You're not being hurt, boy; you've got the
weight," he explained, as though the Monarch would
understand. "If you tear yourself loose you'll bleed
like a pig. Let him pull, Jerrypup; let him wear his
heart out pulling at you, boy. He'll let go without
tearing you by and by."

And something in the calm tones reassured the great
dog. Something in the handpat that was risked down
to him from time to time made him understand after
a while that it was part of the game merely to brace
his legs and wait; and his snarling efforts to break

loose ceased and he began very calmly to endure. It was an hour before Slugs O'Boyle could get his dog to understand that Becky deHavin and the White Monarch of Glenmere were team-working at the game like veterans. But at last it filtered through the Grip's battle-crazed head that he could never throw his enemy or hurt him with the hold he had; and he let go and struck for a better one.

But by now the Monarch had found out why he had been born. Not for the ease of his kennel at the Glenmere Hunt Club; not for the pleasant adulation of the bench or the proud honour of the judging ring; not for romping afternoons with a slim brown girl who had rewards of sweet hilarious waters to offer him after torturing labour; not even for the noble companionship of men like the tall fair one who stood by him now in his great hour—not for any or all of these had his fierce-featured, soft-eyed mother whelped him into the world. But for this night in the stifling, tobacco-laden air, here on this square of yellow tanbark, he had been bred true to his type down through the long centuries since his fathers had pulled down the great Kentish bulls. For here was battle, vicious, snarling and pitiless, and an antagonist that would clash teeth against his in it to the death. And his mighty heart rejoiced as he came into his own.

So when the Grip finally loosed his first hold he found a different dog from the one on which that hold had fastened.

So now, before that gathering of savage men, there raged a furious grim struggle such as the pit had never seen before. For five long hours there came never a pick-up, or scratch, or turn, except that first turn which the inexperienced Monarch had made. Shoulder to shoulder, breast to breast, brisket to brisket, as they reared up on their back legs, fangs to fangs, those two beautiful brutes fought out there under the yellow light their love and joy of death-battle in a contest of infinite courage against infinite courage, and of speed and punishing jaw against overwhelming weight. All other things were equal: condition to endure; strength of limb and wind; valour—all balanced in the scale. Only the one combatant possessed superior speed and a well-nigh decisive power of true punishing jaw; while the other held the vast advantage of being nearly twice his opponent's weight. And, had these unbalanced forces been added to the level beam that weighed their other attributes, the measuring needle would have scarcely stirred.

Weeks of training on the coonskin had in the end forced the idea through the Monarch's heavy skull that he could never hold a grip unless his jaws were filled clean to the back teeth. And so he plodded through the minutes and the hours with never a thought of clamping his untrue fangs on anything, but of trying stubbornly and endlessly through pain and torture to fasten his back teeth upon an enemy possessed of such baffling speed that, at the end of hours of hopeless endeavour, a sickening discouragement came over him. Yet he kept steadily on; and at length a reward came—though he never knew it. Once his ponderous underjaw snapped up on one of the Grip's forelegs. Only the fangs closed over it, and he did not try to hold his grip; but the tremendous muscles of his neck gave his body such a wrenching twist that the bones between those inefficient fangs snapped off before the hold was loosened. And after that the Gas-House Pup gave an exhibition of such undying grit that his name survives the game which died, and lives to this day in the legends of the pit. And this is what is said of him: that, with the broken foreleg, the speed of the Grip diminished not a whit, but that he worked on the end of the broken bone as though the leg were a perfect member.

Pity in all that square of men about the pit, there was none. And, in truth, the battle bred no pity— only wonder. The hard followers of that ancient game gathered round those eight-foot squares for another fascination than the acknowledged ones of carnage and utter savagery. They came primarily to see that thing which is perhaps the noblest attribute in dogs and men—unbreakable courage—courage in pain, and exhaustion, and heart-sickening failure after heart-sickening failure; that rose and rose and rose to heights unbelievable within the cruel sides of those old dog-pit squares; and that changed the men looking at it from a combat-thirsty horde of brutes, quiet from police fear and from a sort of shame at what they

joyed in, to an awe-stricken audience, whose silence
was almost that of worship.

"Three o'clock," announced the referee.

Men snatched a squint at their watches unbeliev-
ingly. Five hours had gone by like one.

But now a haze had begun to form in front of the
Monarch's eyes, which only would be dispelled at the
sound of the low voice he had listened to for encouragement and advice through the rapturous hours.
And always that encouragement and advice had been
at hand. Not the least fascinating thing presented
in the pit that night was the dog-handling of Becky
deHavin. Graceful and cool, fearless and kind, fair-
est and least excited when his dog's case appeared the
worst, magnanimous almost to a fault, this dapper and
stiff-shirted man won his way into the heart of the
meanest thug who had his money staked on the Grip.
And his great dog, in his direst straits, always looked
up at him asking what should be done next about the
situation; and at a quieting pat, that somehow could
reach him even through the fiercest turmoil, he would
stay quiet and rest himself under a painful but not
dangerous grip, or at a fiery word would rage like a
lion till he tore himself free from a hold that threatened
to develop perilously.

But the flitting brindled pest was becoming harder
and still harder to attack. The mist persisted strangely
before his eyes despite the clearing voice. The tan-
bark turned from yellow to red with a flood from his

veins that seemed to be inexhaustible; and never a pick-up came to give his handler a chance to try to stanch his wounds. He did not know that the Grip also now swayed and tottered on his legs, and slashed and snapped his heartbreak that he could not find the great dog's vitals, standing, nor could throw him off his feet to seek them out. The charging rushes of his monstrous white enemy had been in the early hours like those battering-ram onsets that used to break through the impregnable guard of KO Pat O'Boyle; and when they had struck the terrier had nearly always broken his hold and rolled him, bruised and battered, over and over till he fetched up with a crash against the pit fence. Well for him that the Monarch had not been fast enough to follow these wild rushes through in time to catch the brindle on his back. As it was every one had shaken him to the heart; and they, together with his hours of tugging at nearly double weight, had worn him down so that his head swayed weakly and his legs bent under him.

But still he managed to evade the weary bulldog's grip.

But for his education to endure the joyless monotony of the training machine, perhaps even the great-hearted Monarch might have wearied of this ghost-fighting and laid his belly on the sawdust, back legs stretched out behind him, frog-fashion, and rolled up his clear brown eyes good-naturedly, begging to be excused from all the worry of it. But he held to the task with a will to see the brindled body lifeless under him, and to hear the voice of his friend and master call out those four sounds that made all labours worth while: "That's a *good* dog!"

At last came a time when the weary animals, whirling into grips, both missed their holds, and each staggered weakly past the other. And then, all in a moment the tide of battle turned heavily against the White Monarch of Glenmere, for here was the opportunity for which O'Boyle had waited patiently through long hours. He stopped like a flash and snatched up the feebly-protesting Grip just as the dogs were lurching together again. Three or four attendants leaned over the pit wall at the Gas-House Pup's corner and, with broad fans, commenced to stir the air to coolness over the panting dog. Water poured down his throat. Slugs O'Boyle, after five hours of steady fighting, had won a scratch. The action had been so furious and fast that neither handler in all these hours had been able to discover a turn of long enough duration to make a pick-out of it.

In a cruelly short half minute no attention had been given the Monarch other than those that aimed to stanch his wounds, for mere physical strength was what he should need for the great test.

"Time!"

Appeared now the wisdom of Shamus McDonald's prophecy, spoken at the very beginning of the fight. At one corner of the square swayed a brindled dog whose eyes still flashed desire for battle, but in whose legs there lived not half the strength that still propped

up the tottering body of the White Monarch of Glenmere. And yet, because of that inexperienced turn
so early in the fight, it was now the bulldog's task to
deliver the gage at the white lime mark so many miles
across the diagonal of that little square.

"Let go!"

Terrance O'Boyle showed the head and shoulders
of his dog between his knees. And no man in that
silent mass but knew that, except for the supporting
hands under his chest, the Grip would have toppled
over where he stood.

But all support was now taken away from the White
Monarch except the support of a dim beloved voice
that spoke to him some unintelligible words about
losing right. And at a kindly pat of a hand, whose
touch he knew as well as he knew the tones of the
voice, he started bravely on the long journey across
the pit toward a hazy sort of tiger-coated dog which
would not come half that weary way to meet him.

A great rage filled the Monarch's breast.

So now this wraith of a dog, which was so hard to
come to grips with when he was close at hand, would
add to all the other vexations of fighting him unwill-
ingness to shorten the long way between them; yet
he would stand there at that impossible distance and
snarl and snarl as though the combat was still sweet
to him! The cruel injustice of it strenghtened the
Monarch's heart. So be it! If that dim brindled
enemy would not come out to meet him, he, Glenmere
White Monarch, who had ancestral traditions to up-

hold and to uphold him, would go the long road himself; for the lust to stand beside the motionless form of
the tawny foe was still mighty within his weary heart.

Absolute silence—not even the sound of breathing,
for all breaths were held.

Two feet; three—four. The white body tottered
and the hind quarters went down.

Terrance O'Boyle picked up the Gas-House Pup.

"Put that dog down!" the voice of the referee
cracked like a whip.

For the clublike stilts in the Monarch's front still
held the deep chest off the ground and shoved the
great savage headpiece forward slowly, dragging the
hind quarters along. Whispers of mighty sympathy
went up. The air above the bloody pit and the savage
men gathered round it filled with a breath that was
very much akin to prayer. All wagers were forgotten.
All thoughts of greed or gain or trickery or unfairness
vanished away before the glory of the thing that was
going on before them. And a thousand rough hearts
hammered a reverence that was not far from the divine
as that broad trail slowly drew its red wet line across
the yellow square. None there but knew that if the
mighty bulldog reached the scratch the fight was a
draw, for neither dog would be able to stand up another
moment after that. And there was none but prayed in
his own hard way that neither of those noble beasts
should have defeat charged to him after those dreadful
hours.

Five feet; six. The scratch line, and the swaying

enemy only a foot away. The Monarch's sturdy forelegs slipped and slid out in front. The brisket touched
the tanbark. The brindled dog that he could slay,
could he but reach him, only a foot away!

The mighty neck stretched forth. The back legs,
rested a trifle during the dragging of them, bunched
up and moved, and the thick white body crawled
along another inch. A weak and eager whimper, with
a stalwart heart's primal longing in it, was the only
sound. Then, ten inches from the white scratch line,
the mighty, mangled head sank down between the outstretched paws, and the breathing and the whimper
ceased; the great form grew very still.

Not a stir of cloth came out of the dark. Terrance
O'Boyle, sure now of the win, made no haste this time
in lifting up the Grip to claim the battle for him.
Had he but thought of what deeds must have been
done through the centuries to turn the designation of
that quiet white beast's breed into a descriptive so
heroic that strong men rejoice to hear it coupled to
their names, he doubtless would have hurried. But
he found it beyond him to resist the vanity of non-
chalance.

And so he never got the Gas-House Dog's paws off
the floor; for, as the very last quiver died in the
white body, two voices spoke in the quiet. The first
was very soft and musically dissonant with the scene.
Some altogether different kind of love than that of
courage must have brought the owner of it into such

a barbarous gathering of men. But the second voice was harsh and rasping and entirely congruous.

"Go swim?" said the musical voice; but the sprightliness of it did not altogether hide the sob.

From some seat high in the surrounding tiers it went down across the reeking air to the yellow rectangle under the hooded lights; and its coaxing invitation won through the mists that were gathering impenetrably about the ferocious, quiet head; for the delicate frayed ears twitched and then came up on top of the massive skull. And the brown eyes, which a thousand men would have sworn had closed forever, opened. At which the second voice, in awed tones that had only reverence, no profanity, in them, expressed what was in the heart of every man watching there.

"By Gawd, that bulldog don't quit when he's dead!" said this grating whisper.

A romping brown-legged pal and the splash of inclosing waters dimly visioned in the White Monarch's parched and weary soul. For a completed task there was always a sweet reward.

A quiver played over the inert muscles. Fronted by stubbornness immeasurable, even disintegration paused—and then retreated; for suddenly, at a mighty summons, there came a great gathering of his passing strength; and the bulldog rose on all four legs at once. He stood—wide-braced, unwavering. That tawny haze of colour right before him—was it the brindle of this enemy who would not come to meet him? Or was it the merry, tantalizing flash of beautiful tanned flesh, coaxing completion of his work? Or both? Without a single faltering step, with never a sign of the weakness that the uplifting of a single paw would have betrayed, the sturdy Monarch made one blind lunge at it. And as the big dog crashed down a sibilant exclamation that expressed emotions not to be set down in writing came involuntarily out of every throat. He lay with his forelegs bent stiffly and grotesquely backward along his flanks, and his back legs stretched out flat behind him, frog-fashion. The referee bent over the still broad body. The noble brute's head had failed to reach the scratch. The sooty nose had fallen short.

But, clear in everybody's sight, just over the white scratch line, upsweeping determinedly out ahead of skull and nose, there rested that very thing which experts had agreed would lose his fight—the prognathous tip of the mighty bulldog jaw.

In deathlike silence the referee stood erect; but when he made his decision no one heard it. Eight or ten blue-coated men, however, nosing round the wrong huge vacant barn, a mile or so off the scent, heard something. An explosive roar of pent-up human voices brought a male chorus to them across the early morning air that sent them scurrying upon a warmer trail.

But long before they reached the right huge vacant barn the best veterinary surgeon in America had ended his instructions to the second and third best of his profession, and had risen up and started to pick the particles of tanbark from his knees. This accomplished, he looked up, and found himself gazing into a very drawn, white, anxious face.

"They both will live," he said, "though I can't tell why. And, by the way, you won't get a bill from me. I've had my money's worth." Which was almost panegyrical, as all will agree who ever came into violent contact with one of his fees.

At once, then, young A. B. deHavin seized the huge shoulder of Mr. Slugs O'Boyle and swung him face about from the little circle that still bent over the two other veterinaries. The ex-light-heavy looked down into steady, pale eyes. Pale eyes looked back steadily; but, as the silence lengthened, they began to gather flame, till at length strong slim fingers closed and supple muscles began to gather inside the right sleeve of a bloody evening shirt. But a graceful boy, whose eyes were still wet with weeping over two dogs, left hovering over them and flung himself so violently upon the bosom of the gory shirt that a cap flew off, and a bushel of blue-black hair tumbled down over the red-splashed cuffs of that same full-dress garment.

Old Bull deHavin snorted his chagrin.

"My luck," he growled. "That's the first time in history that anybody in trousers ever prevented a fight. And me living all these years for the day when I could see one of my sons with a black eye!"

"Fight, fight, fight!" spoke up Nora McDonald out of the shelter of the gory sleeves. "You men! Do you never get enough of fighting? And do we always get what strength is left for loving after your fights have taken the best of you?"

Her daddy's eyes glinted wisely.

"No and yes to you, Nora machree," he answered, "much to the benefit of the world you're livin' in."

And A. Beckwith deHavin, III, by way of proof that Daddy McDonald's answer was correct, had never stopped the glare he was shooting into the eyes of Slugs O'Boyle.

"This girl has seen enough of male brutality to-night," he said; "but she's going to see some more if it takes you much longer to say it."

And to show that there actually was one thing in the world he would rather do with his arms than that which then kept them occupied, he loosened one of them from about the prettiest shoulders on the big-time circuit.

Terrance O'Boyle looked into the pale hard eyes again. He studied appraisingly the slim, well-knit body, which the will back of those hard eyes was about to drive against his overwhelming bulk; and the curl straightened out of the line of his thin lips. No fear showed in his eyes; only conviction. Gradually a different kind of curl came over his mouth— one that caused that disengaged, tense arm to relax and to go back where it belonged; for the curl became a sure-enough smile that made even the brute face of Slugs O'Boyle pleasant to look at, principally because it brought out the hidden resemblance to Brother Pat, who was standing, an interested spectator, close at hand.

"And if he falls down at the trimmin' of you, Terry," remarked Brother Patrick, "I'll finish the job for him."

But Terrance, with the fine big smile still suffusing his face, stuck out a flipper of a hand to the third Beckwith deHavin. That young man once more disengaged a very busy arm.

"My dope's all wrong," admitted Slugs O'Boyle. "Beg yer pardon! I believe you stiff shirts kin lose right."

A. Beckwith deHavin, II, looked toward his son, and his heart hammered a tune. "Old Bull deHavin," it said in his ear, "what you're gazing at now is a fighter. And look at his arm—not the one shaking hands, but the other; it's wrapped round his woman!" The president and general manager of the Interborough Gas Company stabbed his elbow democratically into the fat ribs of the I. G. Co.'s stable boss.

"I guess the brindle isn't all bred out there yet!" he chuckled.

Shamus McDonald returned the stab.

"Better to play a thing like that safe, A. B.," he said. "But I've the idea in my head that Nora Kolananikau won't be after doin' her divin' stunt alone this winter. It'd be no surprise at all to her Polynesian father if she'd decide to team up with her sister again in a different act entirely."

And he winked at his boss a Brobdingnagian sort of wink, as one who would impart that, by the use of a marvellous worldly wisdom, he has arrived at certain astute conclusions.

THE END